Lunch

Hour

by Jose Antonio Ponce

Printed in the United States of America

For information, please address the author at PO Box 6552, Albuquerque, New Mexico, 87197.

This book may be purchased for educational, business or sales promotional use. For information, please contact the author at the above address.

Second edition

This is a work of fiction. The characters in this book are fictitious. Any similarity to any persons living or dead is coincidental and not intended by the author.

Acknowledgement is made to speakwithoutinterruption.com where the following stories were first published in a slightly different form:
Background Action; King of Pain; Paper Joe; West of Town; Pagans; Fat; Angels We Have Heard; Soccer and the Decline of Western Civilization; Pod People; Sponsor; Jazzed; Old Fart; What a Long, Strange Trip It's Been; Lunch Hour

Library of congress Cataloguing-in-Publication Data
Ponce, Jose Antonio
Lunch Hour / by Jose Antonio Ponce
ISBN 978-1461017950
1.American wit and humor. 2. Short stories

10 9 8 7 6 5 4 3 2 1

*

For my wife Kathy

*

Contents

Forward

I have been writing since I was thirteen. Poetry and songs, mostly, but some short stories and essays as well. Like most writers, I started out telling stories about me and how the world affected me and what I would do if things were different, how I would make the world better.

As a kid, I shared the things I wrote with girls to get them to like me. Later in life, I thought myself to be *über* creative and tried my hand at everything, science fiction, romance, horror, comedy, drama and the occasional screenplay or novel. Looking back on that stuff, (I save *everything*) I sucked.

I simply couldn't understand that the world did not revolve around me. I bounced from job to job and did lots of things to draw attention to myself, including playing music and doing standup comedy for a living. Eventually I learned to just shut up and observe and discovered that most people are waaaaay more interesting than I could ever hope to be.

What I have here is some things that I wrote on my lunch hour at work. I don't have much of an attention span and I found that an hour is just about the right amount of time to sit down and compose. More than that and my mind will start to wander.

This book took a long time to come to fruition. Some of the stories in here are things that actually happened to me with a little embellishment, some are about the way I wish things had gone had I turned left instead of right; some are just stories that make my life seem more interesting than it actually is. Mostly, though, it's all still about me.

90 Days

I sit at my desk
and mark time
in quarterly reports
annual budgets
and long-term goals
my life passes me by
in ninety day cycles
that's the terminus of my password
it must be changed
from one secret word to another
letters, symbols and numbers
and cannot repeat
for ninety days

Background Action

I spent two very long days on the set of the movie "Paul" written by and starring Simon Pegg and Nick Frost some time ago. I had not been on a movie set in nearly twenty-five years, when I was cast as the "Mexican" in a western mini-series. With my intention to find more work in the film industry, I decided that spending time on a movie set to refresh my understanding of the film process might be a good idea. An opportunity to work as an extra presented itself and so I took two days off from my job to work the crowd scenes.

Some of the scenes take place at the San Diego Comic Con. I was one of those non-descript people you see in the crowd scenes. We were invited to participate by the film's production company who offered to pay a fixed dollar amount to my favorite charity for every person I could bring on set. We ended up with only a handful of people, but it was an enjoyable, if exhausting experience.

Since we were not pre-cast as extras, we merely had to show up on the first day of the shoot and register. Easy Peasy. As I stood in line, I noticed the odd assortment of people. There were couples, young and old, and the type of people who seemed less than disciplined; students, retirees, part timers and the chronically unemployed. Because these crowd scenes were supposed to take place at Comic Con, there were also a number of extras dressed as their favorite sci-fi characters including Darth Vader, a cadre of Imperial storm troopers, a miniature Boba Fett, both a youthful (Episode 3) and aged (Episode 4) Obi-Wan Kenobi, a Wookie, an X-Wing pilot and no less than seven Princess Leia's (the scantily clad chained to Jabba the Hutt version, one of them, male). There was Star Trek TNG's Captain Picard and several "classic" Star Trek crewmen (and women) including Yeoman Janice, a green skinned Orion slave girl and an assortment of other sci-fi and fantasy characters including Frodo from the Lord of the Rings and a guy in a cheesy homemade Robocop outfit. I felt strangely out of place not being in some sort of costume.

Once we had signed our release forms and had our continuity photos taken, we were taken to holding, a large hall ringed by makeup and wardrobe personnel and plied with snacks of all sorts. The wardrobe people went through our clothing (we were asked to bring three changes of clothing) and dressed us appropriately. They left me as I was.

During the orientation, those professional extras listened politely but with the air of those airline passengers that have flown a thousand times. They already know where the emergency exits are. The rest of us took notes. After the orientation, we were led into a theater for some crowd reaction shots, people wildly cheering as their sci-fi heroes took the stage. We were then sent back to holding while the crew set up the next shot. We found our seats again, (extras tend to be notoriously territorial) and waited for the next scene to be shot. I noticed that people acquainted with one another socially or by common interest sat together. Those extras that had met previously on other sets chatted with one another about their experiences on this film or that. I also noticed that people grouped themselves by character. All of the Star Trek people hung together as did the Star Wars and Lord of the Rings people.

There were also subsets. All the guys playing security guards sat together. At first, I thought that they actually were security, but after the first scenes of the day, it was obvious that they were extras as well. The demons, wizards and warlords sat separately, presumably plotting the demise of the gentle souls on a quest. Others not in costume but with a common interest sat discussing their favorite characters or the deeper meaning of the World of Warcraft. The Princess Leia's chatted like sorority sisters and the Imperial storm troopers stood watch over us all.

I had heard about this happening on the original Planet of the Apes film. Once in costume, between takes, the apes broke into separate groups, as did the orangutans and the gorillas. People with no common interest out of costume would sit and talk with each other while in costume. I asked the casting director about this at party later in the week and she said that it's a pretty common occurrence on movie sets.

My friends and I, who have little interest in sci-fi or fantasy, sat around trying to determine who still lived with their parents and who had a job in the tech industry. I encouraged the girls to flirt with the geekiest looking guys on the premise that this would give them confidence with the opposite sex, but they just thought I was being cruel.

After much socializing and more food, we were ushered into the large hall where production assistants set about positioning us for the crowd scenes in the movie. We were given some simple directions. We were to follow the path the PA set us on and react to our surroundings with wonder. We were to engage in noiseless faux conversations with one another so as not to intrude on the dialogue. "Some people like to repeat the phrase, peas and carrots," one PA told us.

Once placed in "first position", we would rehearse a scene for the cameras and principle actors, making sure that the angles were correct and that we were moving with the required energy. Each rehearsal and subsequent take would begin the same. The director would shout "picture up", followed by "rolling", a pause, then "background action. This was our cue to move. The PA staff echoed each command and after the "rolling" command someone would shout, "Quiet please". Once we began moving, the director would shout "action" to cue the principle actors.

Each extra, dedicated to his or her craft, would walk and engage in eerie silent conversation with complete strangers, like the mall zombies in George Romero's "Dawn of the Dead". We walked and mimed until the director yelled "Cut" and then the clarion call of every PA, "Back to first position!" or "Back to one!" would bring us dutifully to our starting points. From above, it must have looked like those microscopic photos of the bloodstream, as the flow of blood momentarily courses backwards through the veins toward the heart with each beat.

Each scene was filmed several times, with a few minor changes here and there for enhancement, I assume. It was odd, meeting the same strangers over and over, having the same whispered fake conversations. I took to trying to make my friends laugh with odd comments or letting out a string of curse words just to spice things up. It was a little like the Phillip K. Dick story, 12:01, in which a man lives the same day over and over, making just a few adjustments here and there, hoping to change the end result, but always repeating the cycle. In the end, he shoots himself in the head to stop the process only to awake to the terrifying realization that he is stuck in this loop, forever. (The lighter "Groundhog Day", was based on this very dark tale.) I wondered to myself if we would be out of focus for these shots, or would I be able to pick myself out in the actual film.

There was a quick break for lunch and then back to holding where we waited to be movie stars again. For the next scene, only a hundred people were taken. The more experienced extras knew that this was often the case and so sat closest to the entrance of the hall. They were chosen more often for scenes and were assigned to a team, giving them more face time. Those who rushed to the call were often disappointed and taunted by the team members.

Life as an extra is a lot of waiting around, unless you're willing to do what it takes to get on camera. Lobster girl (a girl dressed as a lobster) was in nearly every scene as were the princess Leia's and storm troopers. My cousin Frank, who's never been able to hold a job in his life, loves being an extra and casting directors love him. He'll do anything they ask. In one movie, he had live maggots dumped onto him as he lay through an hour and a half of takes as a mangled body. In another instance, he spent two hours draped over a barbed wire fence and in still another, he spent nine hours lying in a mud puddle.

As the day progressed, whole groups of people slept, read books, played cards and made repeated trips to the snack table. There was a lot of time to people watch. More than once, I caught myself admiring the rear end of Princess Leia only to discover too late that I had been looking at the drag Leia.

By day two the crowd had thinned out a little, with some of the volunteers only able to take one day off of work. The first timers who returned were more prepared, bringing blankets, pillows, laptops, DVD players and games. There was a rugby team practicing their scrums and a few guys tossing around a Frisbee in an empty ballroom. Everybody's energy seemed to wane a bit during the scenes and the production assistants did their creative best to keep us animated. One of the PA's led willing participants in an impromptu conga line. Another gathered us together for a raucous and racy version of the Hokey Pokey. ("Stick your tushy in, stick your tushy out..."). After two days, it wasn't that weird to be standing at a urinal next to Darth Vader wondering if he was breathing hard because he was still in character or if he was just having prostate problems.

Sitting so near to so many people in holding, it was hard to not listen to conversations. Among those people who make sci-fi and fantasy their passion, I heard arguments about people traveling to and from other dimensions, discussions about continuity errors in films, especially involving time travel and the sharing of the latest technologies used in film to make the fantastic seem real. I was privy to a conversation between a white man in his early forties and a young Asian girl no older than twenty-three. They discussed their favorite movies, books and films with no barrier between them. Their age, class, culture and income did not matter here. They were simply fans.

Some discussions centered on the film itself. After spending that much time on the set, many of the extras became directors themselves, discussing camera angles, crane shots, continuity and speculated on the plot. Many talked about their own screenplays.

The two days progressed pretty much the same from that point on. Eat, read, act, read, eat, sleep. I even smoked a couple of cigarettes just to break up the monotony. At the end of the shoot, the extras lined up for their pay slips, giddy with excitement and a little sad that this adventure was over. This was what they called a good shoot. The atmosphere was pleasant, the primary actors were accessible and the extras were treated with respect. I never heard anyone, from the director to the casting assistants yell at anyone. I have been on some rough shoots, and this one was, by far, the best. I'd do it again, maybe when I retire or if I become unemployable.

King of Pain

Gary sat there on the end of the king sized bed, his back to the sleeping beauty beneath the covers. He slumped, defeated, in his plain, white boxers staring at his reflection in the TV and taking stock of all that he had just thrown away. He had on an unbuttoned stockade shirt. At least that's what they used to call the denim colored cotton shirts he favored. He always wore them with the sleeves rolled halfway up his forearm. It was a style he picked up from his older brother and when he combined it with a cigarette tilted lazily from his mouth, he looked cool.

He was hoping to hide his girth with the shirt should Linda wake up and see him in the light of the morning. He was the color of biscuit dough, with a deep scar running the width of his paunch from an emergency appendectomy 5 years ago. His chest, once hard with soft wisps of fine blond hair, was a cushion now and covered with grey. His hands were scarred from years of concrete work and carpentry and his face had slid into a permanent frown. Yesterday he was 17. Today, he was older than his 50 years.

His marriage was clearly over. He could kiss his house and most of his possessions goodbye. He was sure that he would never be able to go back to work. He would never be able to go back and face those people once they found out where he had been. He would be too ashamed.

His dogs! He was going to lose his dogs! He loved those pups. They were the only things in the world that mattered to him and he was surely going to lose them to his wife. There was no way she would let him keep the boys with the leverage this would give her in a divorce.

Linda lay sleeping under the sheets, one leg out to regulate her body temperature. Her blonde hair curled onto the side of her face and her breathing steady. She was beautiful. He had never known a time in his life when she was not beautiful. Nothing about her had changed since high school, he thought, except that she had become sexier with the arrival of her wonderful breasts in her early 20's. She had also had a small bump on the bridge of her nose removed through rhinoplasty. He used to probe that tiny imperfection, the only one he could find on her body, with the tip of his index finger as she slept. He missed not having it there. She slept as if she had just drifted off after another ordinary day. Nothing on her face gave away what they had done. They had run away together...again.

How foolish and impulsive. How stupid and selfish. He knew better. He was supposed to be a grown up. He had responsibilities. Jesus, what was he going to do now? He felt the way he did on that day when his father caught up with them all those years ago, timid and gutless. He half expected his father's squat, muscular frame to burst through the door any minute, his red face even more flush than usual and drag him out to the truck.

Linda was out of his league, and he had known this from the day they were first introduced. She was just out of high school and he had a year to go. It was a chasm he was sure would keep them separated forever, but she treated him as if he were anyone else. He was in love with her from that moment on.

Tall, slender, blond and gorgeous; smart, witty and with attitude to spare she always did whatever she wanted. She loved to drive fast and had that reckless independence he hoped might rub off on him and accelerate his journey into manhood. Gary had always done as he was told. His father's word was law. No debate, no negotiation, no flexibility. His father knew what was best for his sons just as his father had known what was best for him. Dreaming was not encouraged. It was time wasted that could better be spent learning or earning. Any dream could be purchased once you had learned how to make a living.

While Gary was having responsibility pummeled into him by his father, Linda was bucking her own father's authority. He was a retired Master Sergeant and he handled his daughters with the same firm military hand that he extended to his sons. All of his children were expected to conform, and so, of course, none of them did. Linda's oldest brother rebelled with drugs, the second son withdrew, her sister and younger brother lost themselves in a series of destructive relationships. Linda developed an uptown wild streak as if to set herself apart from a family that was, in her opinion, too suburban. She was reckless, stayed out late and adopted friends she knew her parents would neither approve of nor encourage her to keep.

Gary was one of those boys. His father was a contractor. Gary was younger than her by a couple of years, scandalous to her peers but especially to Gary's parents. What could this older girl possibly want with their underage son? Linda's parents, while cautious, had learned by then not to bridle her because in their experience, she only stood closer to the edge when called to task. She would lose interest in this boy soon enough if they just left her alone.

Gary had never had any girl show such an interest in him. She teased him ceaselessly before allowing him to kiss her. She grew to love his need for her and impatient with his the slow pace of his experience. She taunted him into breaking his father's rules. She was his confidant, his confessor, his Buddha, teaching him things about life he knew existed but never understood or even hoped to experience. She imposed her will with a silken lash. Their romance was rash, uncontrolled and brilliantly orchestrated by her.

For months he had been complaining about living at home with his parents. He dreaded coming home from school to endure his father's grilling about where he had been. He felt his parents' expectations of him and the pace at which he was to achieve unreasonable. He was never good enough for his father in any way, as a student, as a young man or as a son. He wanted to run away to someplace where he could be his own person, a place where he could make mistakes on his own.

As they sat in the car on the western edge of the city, Gary lay with his head in her lap and whimpered that he wanted to run away, hoping that her sympathy would lead to sex. She stopped stroking his crisp, blond hair and snapped at him, "Then why don't you?" This was not the response he had been hoping for. He searched for an answer. "Let's go right now." she continued. "You don't have to go home." She pushed him aside and sat him upright behind the wheel of his Dodge Dart. "Let's go." she urged.

What to do now, he thought. She was acting like his mother, telling him to make up his mind. She was forcing him to choose between acting like a timid seventeen-year old boy and becoming a decisive male. Which person did she want? Did she want him to choose between her and his mother, between family and love? If he made the wrong choice, he might as well kiss her goodbye right now. He pulled a pack of Camel filters out of his denim shirt and lit one, as if to give him time to think. He started the car, put it in drive and pulled out onto the highway heading west.

They didn't get very far. Neither had very much money, and in truth, Linda was just causing trouble. She just wanted to see how far he would go. When he didn't come home, Gary's dad called a couple of his friends that were on the state police force and had them issue a watch for the car. He drove out to where the cops had stopped them and dragged Gary into the truck. He grabbed hold of Linda, who refused to go. She was an adult, after all, and she didn't have to go anywhere she didn't want to. He left her and the car there with the police. She called a friend to come and get her.

Linda and Gary continued to see each other, but under the watchful eye of Gary's parents and with the restrictions they placed on him, it would not be the same. His longing for affection and his new found confidence in himself led him to a series of brief relationships. He used his experience with Linda to turn a sympathetic ear of one romantically inclined girl after another. His Romeo and Juliet-esque story turned out to be the perfect pickup line. He'd romance these girls, sleep with them and after a time they would grow tired of his wistful memories of Linda. Gary and Linda broke up about a year after running away together.

Gary blamed his parents for his loss. He blamed Linda for making him choose. He felt like she had forced his hand. In truth, he did what most young men who discover that they can be loved do. He moved on to see how much love he could find. It was his stepping out on Linda that doomed them. There was no shortage of men who wanted Linda for themselves who told her about his other girls.

As the years passed, Linda and Gary drifted in and out of each other's lives. She married and divorced a number of times. She always married impulsively for reasons they both could only speculate about. Gary moved out of state, away from his father's presence but not his influence. He married a young, pretty Asian woman and gave her everything she wanted.

Gary and Linda had lunch on those occasions when he traveled home to visit his parents and he still told her all of his problems. He made excuses to come home just to see her. He loved her in a way he could not explain to her or to himself. He knew everything about her, much more than he knew about his wife. He had rolled his emotions up in an effort to appear aloof, uncaring. He pretended to be a man who did only what he wanted to do, a mirror of the person she had always been. They flirted easily without resolution. He longed for her and the excitement she had brought to his life. When he found himself depressed, she eased him through it. When she did something stupid, she asked for his opinion, his male perspective
.

Running away with Linda was the only unplanned thing he had ever done in his life. Now, 33 years later he had done the same thing with the same girl largely for the same reasons. Looking back on a lifetime of stolen moments with Linda, he realized that this what he had wanted all along. To be alone with her one more time. To break away from the capitulation he had chosen to make his existence. When he was 17, he had endured the beating of his life from his father. Now he would take an equal amount of punishment from his soon to be ex-wife and her lawyer.

He sat there, silently contemplating the calluses on his hands. He had learned from his father. He had worked hard, started his own construction company and saved every penny. He was closer to retirement than almost any of his peers. His hands were the proof of what he had accomplished through sheer will and misery. Now, he would have to start over again. This choice would ensure that he would never see the day when his hands would not be leathered by labor.

He pulled a cigarette from the half empty pack in the pocket of his shirt and lit it. He glanced back at Linda, still sleeping. She dreamed without anything to disturb her. She was beautiful, and that would save her as it always had. Her husband, with reservations, would take her back. Her co-workers and friends would gossip about her affair and speculate about the man she ran off with. The incident would confirm, for some, her favored status among men. It would be explained to her children that their mother had just needed a vacation from the stressful life that was the balance of work and family. There would be no consequence for her. Gary would again take the beating for her, because he loved her.

With apologies to "Flat Stanley", please meet…

Paper Joe

Joe hated his job. As a telemarketer, he sat in a small cubicle all day long bothering people on the phone trying to get them to buy things that nobody needed. All day long, Joe's boss yelled at him, "Sell more Joe! Sell more!"

Although he was good at his job, he never made enough money to do the one thing he loved most. Joe loved to travel. He loved the freedom of going different places and doing different things.

One day, while Joe was on his ten-minute coffee break, a rather large co-worker offered Joe a donut. "C'mon, Joe," he said, "thing's aren't all that bad. At least we have jobs."

Joe reached from his chair up to get a donut. Just then, Joe's boss came up behind Joe's co-worker yelling, "Break time's over! Back to work!" He startled Joe's co-worker so badly that the co-worker fell on top of Joe.

"Oh, no!" the co-worker cried, "I've fallen on Joe"

"Ummph!" said Joe.

"Back to work!" yelled the boss. It took two of Joe's other co-workers to get his large friend off of Joe. When they did, they made an amazing discovery. Joe had been squashed flat as a piece of paper.

"Call 911!" said someone.

"Wow! He's really flat." exclaimed a co-worker.

"Flat as a piece of paper." said someone else.

"Whoa!" said Joe. "What a trip!"

"What's going on here?!! I said get back to work!" yelled the boss again.

"Joe's been squashed flat!"

"Flat as a piece of paper." said another co-worker, again.

"Well, staple him back to his chair and glue his hand to the telephone and get back to work!"

"What about my injury?! cried Joe. Surely this can't be good for me?

"Your injury is your problem. Keeping the phones ringing is my problem. If you don't get back to work in two minutes, YOU'RE FIRED!!!"

"I'll sue!!!" yelled Joe. I'll sue you for every penny you've got!

"Oh yeah?" said the boss, narrowing his eyes and threatening Joe with his cigar. "I'd like to see you try."

Joe found an attorney in the phonebook under the heading of "Accidents". His name was Silas and he could see right away that Joe had a case, and one that could offer a big payoff. He told Joe that he would take on his case on a "contingency" basis. That meant that he would get exactly one half of whatever Joe got in compensation for his injury. "The harder I work," Silas explained, "the more money we both make." That was quite all right with Joe.

Joe's attorney filed a motion with the court asking for fifty million dollars. They said that the telemarketing company had been negligent in providing donuts to the workers for free. It was this negligence that caused Joe's co-worker to become large enough to cause the injury to Joe. Had the company been more forward thinking, they would have seen the potential for harm that this environment of free donuts created.

Silas and Joe made quite an impression on their first day in court. Instead of walking into the courtroom like a normal person, Joe's attorney brought him into the courtroom in a large manila folder. It was requested that all of the doors and windows to the courtroom be kept tightly closed so that Joe wouldn't blow away. Special furniture had to be brought in for Joe so that he could sit comfortably. Periodically during the trial, Joe would curl up like a pirate map and his attorney would have to request a recess so that Joe could be ironed out.

Joe's attorney painted a gloomy picture of what life would be like for Joe from now on. He would never be able to go out on a windy day for fear of becoming a kite. He would not be able to frequent diners that had an open flame grill, as he was now highly combustible. He would no longer be able to work. Even the most menial of jobs presented hazards to him in one form or another.

Worst of all would be the humiliation. He would never be able to go anywhere without people staring at him. Even now, attorney Silas said, children taunted his client with shouts of "There go Paper Joe! There go Paper Joe."

The telemarketing company's attorneys could see the handwriting on the wall. The jury was obviously sympathetic to Joe's plight, with one woman even breaking down into a gentle sob as Joe described how his life had been ruined by his injury. The capper was when Joe offered her his paper-thin sleeve for her to use as a tissue.

In the end, the telemarketing company settled for "an undisclosed amount". It was enough to make both Joe and attorney Silas rich beyond the dreams of Avarice.

After the settlement, Joe entertained ideas about how to spend his newfound wealth. He thought briefly of purchasing the telemarketing company and firing his old boss, but he soon found out that the owner of the company had beat him to it, sending him off with only a box of stale donuts as severance pay.

Joe bought a new home, a new car, a boat and new clothing, all custom made for his flat stature. Still, he longed to travel. He couldn't drive his new convertible from place to place because he might end up blowing away. Air travel might reverse his condition because of the pressurized air in the jet and if that happened, he would have to give all the money back. He got too seasick to travel anywhere by boat and trains and busses were for poor people and he was certainly no longer poor.

And then in a flash it hit him. He would mail himself wherever he wanted to go; after all, almost any place around the world had a post office of some sort. Better yet, he would send himself to all of the luxurious hotels he planned on staying in during his travels. All he would need would be a few hundred custom envelopes of the proper size and several books of first class stamps. "Well," Joe chuckled to himself, "I've always wanted to travel first class.

After visiting the stationary store, the bank and the post office, Joe pulled out a map of the United States and drew a big red circle around Las Vegas, Nevada, a place he had always wanted to visit. Joe carefully packed a few changes of clothing, some stamps for the return trip and a flat bundle of cash and travelers checks into the oversized envelope. "Sin City, here I come!" he said as he sealed himself into the envelope and leaned himself against the mailbox.

"Whoa," moaned Joe as he crawled out of the envelope at the end of his daylong trip. "I'll have to remember to write FRAGILE in red letters on the envelope the next time I travel." A startled hotel manager simply stared at Joe as he slid out of the envelope. "You're finest suite, my good man," said Joe handing the manager a $50.00 tip, "and send up some champagne." The manager had little choice but to comply as hotels in Las Vegas are designed to cater to the rich and odd.

Once he had settled into his room, Joe decided to see the town. As he left the lobby and strolled into the casino, he met some very friendly ladies. They seemed to know that he was there to have a good time and they offered to help him enjoy himself. Together they played roulette, Black Jack, Craps, Keno and most of the slot machines.

Vegas is a wonderful place, Joe thought to himself. All the drinks were free, the girls were friendly and the other casino patrons paid no attention to his obvious flatness as if it were the most normal thing in the world. This was the place to be. The last thing Joe remembered were the girls ordering more champagne from room service.

"Whoa!" said Joe when he woke up the next afternoon. "I guess that champagne went to my head but I must have had a good time because the room is a mess."

Joe's clothing was scattered everywhere, there were more than a few empty champagne bottles and the dresser drawers were all opened. The girls were nowhere to be found and all of Joe's money was gone, including his traveler's checks. Joe called down to the front desk to report the incident. "What can I tell you sir?" the manager sniffed, "It's Vegas."

Joe called his banker at home and had him send enough money to pay the hotel bill and for postage home. "Never again!" said Joe.

Joe decided that his next trip should be somewhere more sedate. Joe decided to visit one of the great theme parks in California. He booked his reservations at the theme park hotel, slipped some casual clothing and cash into an envelope, stenciled FRAGILE in bold, red letters across the front of the envelope and mailed himself off to the land of fun.

His trip this time was better. When he arrived at the hotel and slipped from the envelope in the mailroom, no one noticed Joe except someone dressed in a large dog suit that was pre-occupied with removing his head so that he could have a cigarette. "I like your costume." the man/dog said, "It's pretty original and that's what they go for here. The pay's not great, but it's all the fast food you can put away, although it looks as though you probably have to watch your weight."

Joe ignored him and strolled up to the hotel desk, but before he could get a word out, he was shooed away by a woman in what could only be described as an aging princes costume. "Away with you now." She said in a grand thespian voice. "You should be out entertaining the guests."

"I am the guests!" said Joe.

After checking in, Joe decided to try some of the rides at the theme park. As he strolled along the grounds, people stopped him to ask if they could take their pictures with them. "They must have heard of me," Joe thought to himself, "and my famous court case." He did find it odd that parents of small children told Joe that he was their favorite character or that they loved his cartoons.

Riding some of the rides made Joe dizzy, while others, got him wet. At one point he flew out of the roller coaster, but floated down to the boardwalk as gently as a feather on the breeze. On one or two occasions, Joe was mistaken for part of the scenery and several times he was told to get back to work by people who seemed to be in authority. At the end of each day's fun, Joe would go back to the hotel and relax. "This is much better than Vegas," Joe reflected as he sat staring out at the glittering theme park from his balcony. "All of the people are so friendly and everyone here seems to know who I am. Some even seem to think that I have been in the movies. This must be what it's like to be a celebrity."

On his last day at the theme park, as he checked out of the hotel, a very stern looking man asked to see him in his office. "What is your name!" the man demanded.

"Joe Smith" said Joe. "Why do you ask?"

"I don't think that you are going to work out here. I have a number of reports of you dining with the guests, riding the rides during park hours and you have even been seen coming out of one of the rooms in this very hotel. As you know, it is our policy that employees are not allowed to fraternize with the guests under any circumstances. I'm sure that you feel that your behavior is harmless. You are certainly not the first person to feel this way. I've heard it all before from young men such as you and I find that the best way to handle it is just to cut the deadwood from the mighty oak that is our organization. Believe me, you will thank me for this one day."

With that, the man handed Joe an envelope and dismissed him with a wave of his hand. Joe walked back to the front desk, paid his bill and walked out into the sunshine. He opened the envelope and took out the pink slip of paper that said "TERMINATION OF EMPLOYMENT Reason: Gross Insubordination." Attached to the paper was a check for two hundred dollars made out to Joe with the notation "Final Pay".

"Whoa!" said Joe, "That was weird.

"Who needs amusement parks?" said Joe. "They're for kids anyway. Now Mardi Gras, that's the place to be."

Joe had heard that Mardi Gras was the grandest of times, with all sorts of revelry and fun. He had looked up the event on the Internet and saw people in colorful costumes, giant floats and all kinds of people in different stages of inebriation. The Crescent City, which New Orleans is called, seemed to be a place where people could go and cut loose. Joe was always about cutting loose.

He arrived at his hotel a week before Fat Tuesday, the final day of Mardi Gras. By now he had learned to make his hotel reservations in advance and then have the envelope containing him delivered to his room. This helped to avoid any surprises or confusion in the mailroom. Once he felt himself slipped under the door of his room, he got out and plopped down on the bed and fell asleep. Traveling by post always took a lot out of him.

Joe awoke to a cacophony of voices, music and sounds he had never heard before in his life. There were people shouting and it sounded as if a riot had broken out just outside his window. He got up and pulled the curtains back in an explosion of light. Outside his window was a small balcony and beyond that, Bourbon Street. Joe went out onto the balcony and absorbed the sights, sounds and aroma of Mardi Gras. "Whoa!" said Joe out loud, "Now this is a party!".

Joe found a complimentary bowl of colorful beads on his dresser with a note explaining the custom of tossing them from the balcony to passers by and a mask to wear as part of the celebration. Joe put on the mask, stuffed a wad of hundred dollar bills in his pocket and went out into the fracas.

Out in the street, the world was pandemonium. People were everywhere and it was difficult to move, but Joe was able to slip through the narrowest of spaces to get to where he was going. Several times, someone tried to pick his pocket, but were thwarted by their inability to get their hands into such a tight space without alerting Joe. Joe's first night was an evening of roaming from club to club and barroom to barroom. Even though many of the clubs were filled to capacity, there was always a place where Joe could slip in and the club owners could always find room for Joe's money.

Joe's first night in New Orleans was filled with Jazz, smoke and the oddest collection of characters he had ever seen, and that included his trip to the theme park in California. He met men dressed as women and women dressed as men. He saw people sobbing with joy and hooting with laughter. He saw fistfights and acts of lewd behavior. "Whoa! That's weird!" he found himself saying every ten minutes or so. All of this activity seemed to be something out of a Roman circus. After his first night on the town, Joe collapsed into bed just as the sky began to brighten. "Whoa! What a night!" he mumbled as he drifted off to sleep.

Joe awoke late on Fat Tuesday. He had slept through breakfast and lunch. He ordered room service to bring him some dinner. "I'd like something traditionally Mardi Gras," were the only instructions he gave the kitchen. Thirty minutes later, a waiter arrived at his door with a pushcart filled with Cajun delights.

There were red beans and rice with big slices of sausage, Crawfish and Shrimp *Etouffee',* Jambalaya, small fried puffs of dough called *Beignets* and two desserts: Bananas Foster and Cherries Jubilee. Joe sampled everything and ate his fill as the waiter stood at attention. The waiter then prepared the dessert pan, pouring some liquid into a shallow pan of cherries and ignited the alcohol with a brilliant flash.

"Whoa!" said Joe, "Put that out! I'm highly flammable!"

"Aren't we all during Mardi Gras?" offered the waiter, smugly. Joe tipped him handsomely and sent him on his way.

Joe had noticed the night before that the balconies were full of people throwing beads to the excitable crowd.

Someone in a club told him that the balcony parties were by far the best during Mardi Gras, so he decided to have his own. He called down to room service and ordered champagne, more food and more beads and told the desk clerk to pass the word around that Paper Joe's was the place to be. Once word got out, his room was filled with women as equally delicious and spicy as the food.

The night went by in a blur. Everyone who came to his room draped beads around Joe. "Whoa! Thank you!" Joe chuckled throughout the night. The Roman circus people were everywhere at once, drinking, dancing, laughing and performing for the crowds below. At one point, he was sure that there was a Jazz band in the room and there may have been a squad of police officers, or they might have been people costumed as police.

And then, suddenly, it stopped. The music, the laughter, the noise all came to an abrupt halt. Joe looked out over the balcony and saw a line of police on foot, in cars and on horseback driving the crowd out of the French Quarter. Behind them was a line of street sweepers cleaning up the mountains of plastic cups, cigarette butts, beads and feathers left behind by the revelers. People filed out of Joe's room and their laughter died at the end of the hallway.

Joe watched the sad parade from his window. Mardi Gras was over. Joe decided it was time to mail himself home.

West of Town

She sat and watched the sunset from her and Dale's back porch. She loved the colors. The sun always eased itself over the horizon, like someone sliding beneath a sage quilt and tucking them self in for the night. The sky changed color from a regal gold to orange to salmon to purple and finally to a beautiful midnight blue.

The stars blinked on one at a time at first and then, as the sky grew darker, she couldn't keep up counting them as they appeared. It was so clear out here west of town and she could see the edge of the universe. The Milky Way. Years earlier, author and scientist Carl Sagan had coined the phrase "billions and billions of stars". Looking up into the night sky she realized he had no idea.

Dale brought her tea out to her, a nice warm Earl Grey, English with just a bit of honey. This had become a nightly ritual, as they grew older. It was amazing how many good things had happened to them over the past 50 years. Had they really been together for all that time? Had they really lived their whole lives here? How lucky, Dale thought, they had been.

They had run away together when they were young, against their relatives' advice. They had come to this place illegally, hoping to start over, when they had broken down just outside of this small town. He was young and strong, well muscled and perfect for work in the mines where he met his wife to be. She was a water girl. They were drones and they would never get out of that pit. They would grow old and die there in the red dust. With no future in either their work or their home and without any real family, there was no one to apologize to and nothing to regret leaving behind.

They found their way to the main road and, choosing one direction for no particular reason and walked until they saw something in the distance. Through the fog appeared a dull, pink glow that pulsed more intensely as they neared it. Once they got close enough, they could make out letters beneath a painting of a huge mining machine. At first, they were startled. Had they accidentally returned home? Would they have to go back to the mines?

As the sunlight began to burn off the fog, they could see beneath the sign a building and beyond that, a town grew out of a haze of mountain mist. The building was a small motel. It was typical of all motels in that day, U-shaped with a small courtyard in the center. There was no pool or any other amenities. Still they had never seen anything like this. All they knew was that it looked like a place to rest after their long journey. This was, they believed with youthful optimism, all one grand adventure.

It was very early in the morning. Daylight was just breaking and they were drawn to the window just beneath the pink neon sign blazing the same color as the dawn. They knocked and shouted and finally pressed a small, red button next to the window. A noise much like the sound of the alarm at the mines sounded and a small, dark, East Indian woman appeared in a light blue robe and matching slippers, her hair tied back and sleep still clinging to her face. She asked them a few questions and pushed a registration card through the slot, but they only looked at it in confusion. The couple spoke no English and the small woman could not make head or tails of their language as they made their best effort to explain their situation.

They needed help. He tried to explain that their vehicle had broken down just outside of town. Could she help him? Was there someone who could help them? Could they rest there for a moment until they could find their way back? The clerk, not understanding, continued to ask questions, peering around them to look for a car or someone to help translate. Despite the irritation of being awakened from a sound sleep, she sympathized with them. She knew what it was like to be stranded. She knew what it was like to be dark skinned in this country. Even after twenty years of working, surviving and succeeding here, people still made fun of her accent. She saw the hope and desperation in the couple's small eyes.

Eventually, it became apparent that this was going nowhere. The manager wanted desperately to get back to sleep and so, handed them a key and pointed to a room through a side door that led to the courtyard. She shuffled away and back to bed. The young man and his new bride followed the sidewalk in the direction indicated by the woman until they came to a door that matched the key. After some difficulty, they entered the room that would become their first home in this little town and slept all day and all night.

Early the next morning, the young man found his way back to their vehicle and pulled from it all of their belongings, such as they were. This shabby bit of transport had brought them a long way and through some difficult terrain. It was only good for scrap, now and he saw no point in finding a way to drag it into town. They had only brought with them only the necessities for living along with a few things that had meaning for them and reminded them of home. He wrapped these small cultural icons in their ragged garments, put the bundle on his back in the style of the mines, and headed back to town.

That same morning, the manager knocked on their door. She was now dressed in a light summer dress, a print of orange blossoms. The young man and his bride understood that there must be some form of compensation for their room, but had no local currency to pay the debt. They offered what personal property they had, none of which was familiar to the woman. Despite the language barrier, the woman managed to convey a counter-offer of work in exchange for their accommodations.

This they could do. Yes, they were excellent workers. Handing them a paintbrush and several cans of paint, she mimed the painting process and an agreement was reached. Later in the day, the hotel manager took the young wife with her as they changed linens and freshened up the rooms after people checked out. In the few weeks that followed, they found kindness and opportunity in town.

Within a month, the motel had been repainted, window panes had been replaced and the whole place generally spruced up. The young couple went looking for additional work in town. They had learned enough English to get by. Both had been attentive students of the motel manager. They had picked up a few key phrases like "May I help you?" and "Just a moment. I'll get the manger." They knew how to give directions to the military school on the other side of town and how to explain that they knew little English. After a few weeks, the couple moved out of the motel and into a rooming house. After a few years, they moved into an apartment of their own.

They had hit town at an opportune moment. Many men were returning from military duty, but many of the young men from this small town chose to move to the larger cities, once having seen Europe and places in the South Pacific. A shortage of men made finding work easier and after a number of menial jobs, the young man found steady work at the Rainbow Bread bakery not far from the motel.

The bakery was one of the first mass production bread bakeries in the Southwest. Their trucks delivered baked goods throughout Texas, New Mexico, Arizona and Colorado. The company advertised that it took eight hours to make a loaf of bread. For most folks, it was more convenient to pay 10 cents for a loaf rather than heat up the whole house in the summertime.

The young man started by loading trucks. Sometimes he went with the drivers on the local routes to help pickup the stale bread and deliver fresh. The stale bread was brought back to the bakery and sold to feedlots for cattle, chickens, pigs and a variety of farm animals. Eventually he worked his way into the building and into the actual bakery. It was as hot as the mines of his youth had been, but immensely white and clean.

Along the way, he made friends with other workers at the bakery. These were people of every background imaginable and from all walks of life, young and old, drifters and lifelong residents, men and mostly women. They worked and played together without any thought of where any of them had come from. What mattered most was that they were all here in the same situation and trying to make the best of what they had. They were equal in all things except culture, and that was the one thing they shared with one another. These people became part of the lives of the young couple that had drifted into town that one summer morning in 1947.

Everyone gathered around church events or school sports or community dances. The young couple learned to dance the Polka, the Waltz, Latin, Swing and even how to Square dance, and everyone loved the movies. Every weekend, the small theatre was packed with people. There they could see and hear the news of the day, a serial, an animated feature and a movie. Everything on the screen was so large, so vivid. It was at the movies that the young man and his wife both learned to speak English proficiently. Best of all, though, were the westerns. There was always plenty of action and there was never a moment in the theatre when people weren't applauding or hooting at the movement on the screen. In the westerns, good always triumphed and evil was always vanquished. And it was from these movie heroes that the young couple adopted their American names. When introducing himself, the young man would proudly introduce himself by saying, "Howdy. I'm Dale!", just like the character in the movies.

As the town grew, so did Dale's desire to be more and more a part of the community. Dale was working the line at the bakery and he was now putting his wife through school. They had never felt so free in all of their lives.

Over the years they involved themselves more and more. By the 70's, Dale had become the one of the general managers of the bakery. He was a member of the Elks, the Optimists and the Shriners. He was a Scoutmaster and a Lector in his church. He sponsored kids for Boy's State and Girl's State through the Bakery and had even held elective office as a precinct captain for local elections.

Dale's wife had also become involved. Even though they had no children, she became a member of the PTA. She offered her services at the USO during the Korean and Vietnam wars. She was involved in community theatre as a set dresser and usher, anything she could do to help.

Both Dale and his wife did everything they could to further the cause of their little community and never once thought of going home or leaving the little town. It was this place that gave them opportunity and showed them kindness from the very first moment they had wandered into town. They had a kinship with these people even though they started out as strangers.

Dale often told the story of Mike the Hippie to illustrate his point. During the mid seventies, Dale became line boss at the bakery. He supervised 30 people on the dayshift, among them an old timer named Carl. Carl had worked in the bakery right from the start. Like Dale, he had no formal education and worked his way up to foreman. Carl was a favorite at the bakery. During the lunch hour he would play his banjo and lead people in singing songs.

Carl always went on about his son Mike, who had left town right after high school and had got mixed up with a bunch of Hippies from up north. He had done his best to raise his son and teach him what was important, but his son would have no part of it. He didn't want to end up like his old man, coming home from the bakery every day smelling like sweat soaked bread. Carl was not ashamed of his son, only disappointed that he had chosen to leave town, grow his hair long and search for something that Carl believed was right there at home.

One particularly hot summer afternoon, as Carl moved quickly up the line to help clear a downed piece of machinery, his vision blurred and the fingers on his right hand went numb. His right leg fought against him and he became confused by his surroundings. Carl had had a massive stroke right there on the floor of the bakery. By the time anyone knew what was happening, his brain had been starved of oxygen for so long that he was left a speechless hulk in a wheelchair.

A massive outpouring of affection followed. Dale saw to it that the company paid for all of Carl's medical bills.

Carl's family was inundated with home cooked food, offers of assistance and money. Dale's wife moved in with Carl and his wife for a week to help ease the transition for Carl from the hospital back home.

A week after Carl returned home, a skinny kid showed up in Dale's office. It was Mike, the hippie kid that had so disappointed his father. He had cut his long hair and was there to ask for a job at the bakery. He had come home to take care of his family. Until the day they died, Mike lived at home and took care of his mother and father. He never missed a day of work and he even learned to play the banjo. These were the kind of people that lived in Dale's community.

After twenty-five years at the bakery, Dale retired. He opened a business that offered temp work to anyone that would apply themselves. When there weren't enough workers to go around, Dale would go out and work side by side with the very people he was offering opportunity to. If someone needed a ride to a job site, Dale would drive them there. He often stopped by the job sites to check on his workers and it wasn't rare that Dale and his wife would put a family up for a few days until they could get on their feet. As far as they were concerned, it was just their way of giving back what this town had given to them.

On their fiftieth anniversary together, Dale and his bride decided to go back to the place where it had all started, The Crane Motel. It had once been just west of town, the last motel or the first, depending on your direction of travel. The neon sign depicted the heavy equipment version of a hoist or gantry. It was not until years later that the young couple would understand the meaning of this illustration that had so frightened them at first. The crane represented all of the construction that had gone on during the building of the Military school and this had been on of the first motels to house the construction crews. They had placed it on the edge of town so that the decent people of the community would not have to mix with the WPA types that were known to be drifters, thieves and drunkards.

By their golden wedding anniversary, however, the town had grown around the motel. They chose to celebrate there, hoping to re-live their most innocent, modest romantic memories. The motel was different by then. Quiet during the day, it was an anthill of activity at night with people in and out at all hours. The faux velvet bed covers and oddly placed mirrors should have been the tip off of how this once home had finally lived up to its reputation as a seedy rendezvous for local prostitutes and their johns. The couple laughed all through the night.

The sky grew more and more brilliant with each new star. Dale sat down in the chair next to his wife. His last day of work had been more than a month ago. He thought that he would get bored with just sitting back and watching the universe expand, but it never seemed to get old.

They had bought this house west of Roswell ten years earlier and spent most of that time remodeling. Dale had used the workers from his company to refurbish most of it. The town had grown almost, but not quite to the edge of their forty-acre ranch. Their home was near the spot where they had broken down so many years ago. They were light years away from that day now.

Dale saw the lights reflecting off the sage first. It looked like someone coming up the driveway. The shadow of their hacienda loomed large in the bright lights in the front of the house and then there was darkness.

"Hello?" they heard an unfamiliar voice say.

"In the back!" yelled Dale. The crunching of street shoes found their way around the wrong side of the house. Dale thought he heard someone curse as they stumbled in the dark. A young man dressed in black appeared at the base of the porch steps.

"Are you Dale?" the stranger asked.

"I am." Dale said.

"Kind of primitive out here." the man joked, looking around.

"We like it." said Dale in a matter of fact tone.

"How long you folks lived here?" inquired the man.

"Long enough." said Dale. "Are you a census taker or something?"

"Nothing like that." the stranger replied.

"Can I get you something?" asked Dale's wife. "A cup of tea?"

"No thanks. You know, people have been looking for you for some time."

"What people?" Dale inquired.

"Your friends. Your families. I was hired to find you, but as you know, the universe is a big place. When you ran off like that…well…people…."

"People what?" questioned Dale.

"Well, people assume things, like maybe you were kidnapped Mrs. Evans or maybe you were, you know…." He drifted off again.

"Hardly." she laughed, a little embarrassed. "As you can see, it's just the two of us."

"Is there something I can do for you, mister?" Dale said suspiciously.

"Hey," the man said defensively throwing up his hands, "I was just hired to find you, not to bring you back. People just want answers you know. The just want to know if you're alright."

"Why of course we're alright!" Dale's wife said. "Look around you. Doesn't it look like we're all right? I mean…we have everything we've ever wanted. Everything we ever dreamed of."

"And everything we could never have gotten at home."

"Well, you know how it is. We all hate to see our citizens leave home. Everyone wants to see us all contribute for the good of the cooperative."

"And end up working in the mines the rest of my life like all of my relations? I don't think so." Dale bristled. "This place has been very good to us. After the crash, we had nothing. The people of this town took us in even though we didn't speak their language. They made us feel welcome, gave us opportunity and let us be individuals, not some part of a collective that discards the weak for the sake of the whole. Here they build up the weak and make them part of the community!"

"Dale." She put her hand on his arm. "What my husband is trying to say is that we have friends here. We have built a home for ourselves, not just a dwelling, but a home."

"Like I said, I'm not here to bring you back. I still think this place seems kind of quaint, but to each his own. If you'll just place your identifying marks here." The stranger held up an electronic notebook and a small round pad. He handed the small pad to Dale who unbuttoned his shirt to reveal a small logo on his left shoulder. He pressed the round pad to the mark without taking his eyes off of the man. The round pad glowed brilliantly. Dale passed the pad on to his wife who did the same. She handed the pad back to the man.

"If you'll excuse me, I'm required to read this to you." the stranger said formally, indicating the notebook. "You are the sons and daughters of your home world from birth until death. We cherish our children and believe that they make us stronger as a whole. Our community is less significant without you but we understand the nature of youth and believe that one day you will return to the place of your birth. You will always be welcomed home."

Dale seemed to soften a little. "Like I said, we like it here. But should we ever truly be needed, we'll come home."

"That's all anyone can ask for," conceded the stranger. "Now if you'll excuse me, I'll be on my way. I have a long way to go." He stumbled back into the same darkness that he had emerged from. They saw the lights once again illuminate the landscape and watched as a small craft drifted quietly over their home and moved off toward the west before shooting up into the heavens. They sat quietly for a moment.

"Your tea's gotten cold." Dale said, "Let me get you a fresh cup."

"I love you, Dale." she said as he turned toward the screen door.

"I love you, Roy." he said.

Pagans

I go to church every Sunday with my mom. We go to the high mass at 9:00 AM because we like the music, the pomp and ritual. It reminds me of the way that church was when I was growing up. The way church used to be before those Vatican II cardinals got their hands on it.

I'm like most Catholics, very pious with many sins. My mom and I always show up early to mass, not early enough to pray the full rosary, but early enough to catch the last one and a half to two mysteries. We don't want to be lumped in with the overly pious Catholics. We do, however want to be the "we're-more-pious-than-you" Catholics for all of the people that come in at the last minute or, worse, after the mass begins.

Again, like most Catholics, I am very judgmental. I frown at people who come in late. I'm bothered by the parents who allow their children to snack or color or play with toys during the mass, rather than teaching their children the importance of being attentive in church. It's true, that I have never had really young children to look after during mass, but surely, any parent should make the effort. When we were children, we took up a whole pew as a family, with my father seated on the center aisle and my mother seated on the outside aisle with the five of us children between them No one of us was ever out of swatting range and if you misbehaved, you could expect a tart slap to the back of your head.

And the way some people dress to come to church. You would think that they had just dropped by as if the holy mass were another shop in the mall. All sorts of people wearing jeans and tee shirts, shorts and flip-flops, NFL jerseys…I tell you, it is scandalous sometimes the way people dress. Young girls and their mothers now come to church all tarted up, with their pierced belly-buttons showing. Worse than that are women who come dressed in tank tops and have no business showing off their muffin top stomachs overflowing their too tight jeans. I mean, even if it were appropriate for church, it's just in bad taste overall.

Now some people will tell you that Jesus was a come as you are guy, which is true. He met with people in crowds and one on one and never looked for their designer labels or asked them about where they were from or what they were about. Hello!! He was Jesus and he already knew everything about them. He knew what was in their hearts and he knew if they were sincere. He *knew* the rich man would never give up his wealth to follow Him before He even set the condition. Me on the other hand, you have to prove your sincerity to me by not chewing gum or talking during the offering or not leaving before the mass is over.

I tell you, <u>that</u> is my biggest pet peeve; people who wait until the priest's back is turned and then bolt for the door as if the building were on fire. These are usually the same people that come in late and try to move me from the end of the pew so they can make a hasty retreat near the end of the mass. "Hey, I was here before the mass started. I got here with one and a half mysteries left to go in the rosary and that entitles me to an aisle seat. If you want to come in late and have a place to sit, you'll have to squirm by me to the middle of the pew."

Some folks think they're clever. They go to communion and never come back. The just continue down the return aisle out the back door as if they are sleepwalking. For those people in their pew who don't go to communion, it must be as if the communicants were abducted by aliens somewhere between the priest and the pew. They are off being probed and prodded on the way to Alpha Centari with Jesus still stuck to the roof of their mouths. Clearly they have a special deal with the Almighty that allows them to get out before the after mass traffic gets really bad. They don't have to take the time to kneel down and thank God for the gift of communion. I can't go to communion anymore since my divorce, but I at least go up to the priest and ask for a blessing.

I try to participate in every part of the mass. I sing along with the choir. I wouldn't if I had a terrible voice like some people in church. Fortunately, I have been singing for most of my life and am very practiced. Besides, I know most of the hymns by heart, even the ones that aren't in the hymnal. I have sung with a choir or two in my day, and I know exactly how the hymns should be sung. I even know the harmonies. I don't sing too loud so as to be distracting to the choir, but I will sing directly at someone I think needs to pay a little more attention to the mass.

I bow respectfully in all of the right places, cross myself when it is appropriate, sit, kneel and stand when I am supposed to. Some people don't bother to kneel. I understand if you have some physical problem that prevents you from kneeling, but being over the age of 50 does not entitle you to slack off in church. My mother is 84 and she still genuflects getting in and out of the pew and kneels during the consecration.

Even worse are the lazy kneelers. Those people who kneel down and rest their butt on the seat of the pew. Why, you might as well not be kneeling at all. As a matter of fact, why not just sit through the whole mass and forget about kneeling or standing altogether? I'm sure the Almighty would understand.

As I listen to the homily (sermon to you pagans) I try to be attentive. As a biblical scholar, I am well versed in what God was trying to tell us through the Old Testament, but there are so many different lessons that can be gleaned from a single verse or reading so it is always best to listen to what Monsignor has to say. It is his job to break the message down for you. Unfortunately, some people take this time to nap or do their nails or balance their checkbook. I can just see them standing in line at the Pearly Gates…"Let's see…$110.32 minus $18.47…seven from twelve is five…carry the one…"

I see the same people in church every week. There is the family that comes to church together, always dressed appropriately and very respectful. They are my favorites. There is the retarded woman who wears what looks like a Toy Story cowboy hat or a baseball cap. She is usually dressed in sweats and sneakers, but she's retarded and therefore exempt from the dress code.

There is the Sandalman, who comes in every week wearing the same white tee shirt, beige shorts and black leather sandals, even in the winter. He looks like he's going clamming right after church, except we live in the desert. He never turns his cell phone off until they make the turn-your-cell-phone-off announcement, as if he's hoping the rules will change this week. There's Black Woman I Used To Know who always smiles at me and says hello. I still haven't figured out where I know her from, but I think she was married to an acquaintance of mine ten or twenty years ago. She's married to Old Dude, who's got to be twenty-years her senior. I think that maybe she couldn't find any Black male Catholics her own age and had to settle for the Old Dude. He says the mass with a rosary clutched in his hand.

There are two sets of Twins. One, a pair of fossilized brothers with the same balding heads and liver spots in exactly the same place, always dressed in Izod jackets no matter what the weather. The other, late teen girls who do everything that they can to distinguish themselves from one another. One wears her hair short, the other long. If one wears a skirt, the other dresses in slacks.

There's the Waterboy, who always come to mass with his parents, Parkinson's Dad & Mom. Waterboy has the annoying habit of bringing a bottle of water with him in case he gets thirsty during the mass. You would think that he could wait an hour and ten minutes to get a drink. He dresses in the kind of shirt you see on Old Cuban men. Lately, I haven't seen his parents with him and I wonder. Did they have a falling out? Did he decide to stop taking care of them? Did they become too sick to get to church? Did they die? It occurs to me that despite the fact that some of these people irritate me, I have a lot invested in them. On some level, I care. They are my Sunday family.

I wonder about them. Might Be Gay Choir Guy, Rosary Ladies, Midget Usher. I wonder about the single moms, the mixed families and the deacons, priests and acolytes. I wonder about their lives, their families and their futures. I can't help but wonder if they ask themselves, "What's with Pathetic Loser Guy Who Comes To Church With His Mother Every Week?"

Fat

Every moment of every day I am reminded of how fat I am. I weigh 354 pounds. I'm not fat all over, like some people with extra chins and fat, jiggley arms. I am fat mostly in the middle and upper torso. My stomach is enormous and my thighs rub together when I walk.

When I wake up, it is to the whooshing sound of my C-PAP machine, a device that keeps my sleep apnea at bay. Sleep apnea causes a person to snore and to stop breathing once into deep sleep. It gently blows air into my lungs, keeping the soft tissue at the back of my throat from cutting off my oxygen supply.

I have had sleep apnea all of my life, and until I got the C-PAP a few years ago I would fall asleep, stop breathing and wakeup suffocating. It was determined by a sleep study that I was not getting more than 30 seconds of rapid eye movement or REM sleep at any one time. As I got older, I would fall asleep almost anywhere; on the job, while I was driving; in church. For a number of years, I had no dreams because I never quite got into REM sleep. My C-PAP machine allows me to breathe normally and sleep throughout the night. Many people of all shapes and sizes have sleep apnea, but mine is caused primarily by my weight.

Once I am fully awake, I find myself, as always, in the depression in the middle of my bed. I make it a point to turn the mattress frequently, sleep toward the edges of the bed and even sideways on the mattress at times in order to keep the valley in my bed from becoming too pronounced. I have to rock myself a couple of times to roll over far enough to turn off the C-PAP and then roll quickly to the other side of the bed to get up.

I hobble to the shower because the arches on my feet are beginning to wear out, having carried my full weight for so many years. My podiatrist tells me that this has caused a loss of elasticity on the sole of my left foot. During the day, my feet lie flat, even with arch supports. At night, the sole of my left foot curls up slightly and when I first put my weight on it, it rebels. The ball of my right foot has grown calloused and painful because I favor that foot until the arch on my left foot is once again stretched out.

After I shower, I wipe the steam off of the mirror to shave. I only clear a small portion off of the mirror so that I won't have to acknowledge my obesity. I would rather not look at all of that flesh. It just depresses me and I have more disappointment waiting for me throughout the day.

All of my pants are a bit too long for me. This is because I can't stand the thought of my gut hanging out over my belt. I pull my pants up above my waist to the middle of my navel and struggle to button them. The resulting look is that of a stuffed sausage. I spend the rest of my day pulling my pants up every ten minutes or so to keep the cuffs from dragging on the ground. As the seasons change I can see that I have added weight to my substantial girth. My summer clothes fit a little tighter as does my winter wear. I have to replace my underwear at an alarming rate because the friction of my thighs soon puts the leg sections in tatters.

My shirts are all XXX now. I have always measured my size by brand associations, from my mother having to look for the husky label when I was a kid to the signs that announce my size with names like Big & Tall Man, Big Dog and the George Foreman Collection. None of the clothing I wear is purchased without announcement. Everything has to be ordered from special catalogues, segregated departments or off racks that proclaim "Larger Sizes $2 More!"

Getting into my car, I have to take care not to plop into the seat. I have destroyed two such seats in two new vehicles, wrenching the bolts that secure the seat to the adjustable metal frame. This is hardened steel, designed to withstand a violent impact without breaking loose from the floor and impaling the driver on the steering column, but somehow, I have managed to do what the national safety institute could not do in a full frontal collision.

At work, most people tend to treat me with respect. There is the occasional reference to my heft, but no more than my remarking on someone's stature, sexual preference or intelligence. It has taken me 20 years to earn this respect, though. For years I was kidded and cajoled in private and in public.

I have to be careful about where I sit. My office chair won't stay up and I am constantly raising myself up and pressing the handle underneath the seat to bring it back up to full height. I am uncomfortable on most furniture. Chairs are either too small or too fragile for me. Several years ago, I broke someone's plastic lawn chair, and since then I just tell people that I'd rather stand. If a couch is too low, I have a bit of a difficult time getting up.

I prefer tables to booths at restaurants because I usually have to wedge myself into a booth. At lunch, if I drop something from my fork there is no way to avoid having it land on my chest or stomach because they stick out so far. I always carry a clean shirt in the Jeep just in case something like that happens. If I bring a lunch from home, I try to make it a modest lunch so that no one gets the idea that I'm fat because I eat too much. Most days, I skip lunch and hang out with the crew just to prove that I don't really need to eat.

My work sometimes requires me to crawl under consoles, climb ladders, scoot under a vehicle or climb lots of stairs. This gets harder and harder the older and heavier I get. I was never thin. Even at my most athletic, I weighed 185 pounds. When I was in the seventh grade, I weighed 212 and when I got married at 26, I was already pushing 250. Work has always been difficult to do at my weight, whether it was a dishwasher, laborer, roofer, janitor, heavy equipment operator, contractor, roadie or engineer. Most jobs are not designed to be done by someone in my condition. Every day, I am embarrassed by the limitations that my size puts on me.

My doctor told me that it took many years to get this way and that it would take as many years to undo the damage, but I was always this way. I was a chubby baby, a husky kid, fat teen and I have grown from an obese adult into a morbidly obese adult. I know that much of that was my fault. There were times in my life when eating was the only thing that fulfilled me. The act of eating itself was where I found satisfaction. There are moments in my life where I ate so fast and so much that I would very nearly choke.

As a kid, I was scolded by nuns and priests and other adults, reminding me that gluttony was one of the seven deadly sins. It was as if they believed that I gorged myself from the time I went home until the time I went to bed. I was examined by doctors, prescribed pills and put on diets. I have been on the grapefruit diet, the water diet, the vegetable diet, the soup diet, the rotation diet, the tuna diet, the fiber diet and the protein diet. I have fasted, taken in nothing but juices, replaced meals with protein shakes, weighed and measured my food, counted calories, carbs, fat grams and sodium intake. My parents were told that once I hit adolescence, I would thin out as I grew taller. This, too, turned out to be an empty promise.

As an adolescent, I had a friend, Mike Padilla. He was heavy too. I had other friends as well, but Mike and I were *Simpatico.* We suffered from the same affliction. Our weight identified us. We almost reveled in our stature. Together we were the fat ass twins. Other teenage boys made jokes about us and we accepted our roles as enforcers and jesters. Fat boys are always good for a laugh.

One summer, Mike began to thin out. The medical miracle that was promised to me was visited on Mike. As he grew taller, the weight began to drop off of him. He became more popular and even began to attract attention from girls. I have never felt so abandoned in my life. Mike, to his credit, remained my friend. I did all I could to distance myself from him, envying his good fortune and blaming him for my misery. Eventually, we stopped hanging out.

When I got married, I resolved to be a better man. I closely scrutinized my diet. I stopped cooking food in the traditional way and began reading health magazines to find a better, more balanced, diet. I began running a few miles a week. When I injured my knee from the stress running put on my joints, I bought a weight set and eventually joined a gym. I found the perfect form of exercise in weightlifting. It put nearly no stress on my joints, made me feel muscular which gave me so much self confidence that I began taking aerobics classes and adding a variety of aerobics to my exercise regimen. I read weightlifting magazines and adopted the techniques, diets and supplement training of the pros.

But it was too late. My body was aging and resistant to change. Although I built muscle and maintained my heart health at an incredible level, I never lost any of the fat. In fact, I continued to gain fat. My doctor was stumped. Sometimes, I think that he didn't really believe that I was making the effort to lose weight. After all, the results were obvious. Even though I could see the difference that weight training made in the size and shape of my arms, shoulders and legs, it did nothing for my midsection. I had a muscular body buried in a mountain of flab. It made me angry and depressed that I could not lose an ounce of fat. My body fat percentage never dropped below 26% in the 15 years I worked out on a regular basis. Eventually, I stopped going to the gym because I simply could not afford it, but I would have spent any amount of money to lose weight had the diet and training worked.

The worst thing has been the way the weight has made me feel about myself. Every sign, every rule seems to be directed at me. I worry about getting on a ladder that has a 300 pound capacity. I hate to fly because someday, they will ask me to pay for another seat. I avoid all-you-can-eat menus because I'm sure that everyone believes that I can bankrupt the buffet.

Most of all, I get to thinking that the reason some things happen to me is because of my weight. Every girl I didn't get, every team I didn't make, every job I lost always seemed somehow related to my weight. People look at me and believe that I have no discipline, no self-control. If I don't get the recognition I want, I start to think it's because of my weight, as if the cool kids in school won't acknowledge me because it will alienate them from their peer group. Every raise I ask for, every position I seek I feel will come down to a choice between me or someone thin. Given that choice, I have to say, I would likely choose the thin person myself.

It's stressful, being this fat. I am in a constant state of worry about the next embarrassing fat moment; about the next time I break someone's furniture or have to excuse myself because I don't fit at the table or in the theatre seat. There is no lobby for fat people to make venues, airlines and restaurants cater to us and there shouldn't be. It would only call attention to us and we have spent all of out fat lives trying not to be noticed.

Now every day is a challenge just to stay at my current weight. I ride a bike to work most days. It is the only exercise I get. I'm sure that I must look ridiculous and pathetic on the stupid thing. When I come home, I take my shoes off in an effort to bring some relief to my tired, aching feet. I carefully sit down on the couch so as not to break it. I never feel like doing any yard work or housework, although I do the minimum to make the house livable.

At the end of the day, I roll myself back into bed, pile the pillows around me and thank God for getting me through another day. I'm sad because I will never have any more than this. I did this. I wouldn't wish it on anyone, ever. I used to cry, but I don't anymore. I don't always pray, although I should. I pray for those like me and for those who have to live with people like me. I pray that heaven will be a place where I can finally be free. I just want to go home.

I adjust the mask on my face, reach over and press the on button on my C-PAP machine and let the whisper put me to sleep and out of my misery for another night.

Angels We Have Heard

My mother and I go to church every Sunday. It's a nice church with a somewhat conservative message and a mass like I remember as a kid. Although the mass is not in Latin, we still celebrate the mass with all of what people might call pomp and circumstance. There is a processional at the beginning of the mass with incense and at least two deacons in support of the monsignor. We don't skimp on prayer and sing the Gloria, the Kyrie and the responses.

Not all of our masses at the church are like this. The evening youth mass is a high-spirited event with a youth choir, complete with electric bass, amplified guitars, drums and even a bongo boy. The early morning masses are more reserved and the Spanish mass is well attended by all cultures, but my favorite is the high mass mid-morning on Sunday.

People tend to be a bit more…respectful at this mass. They genuflect and bow at the proper times and dress appropriately. They listen attentively to the word of God and don't chatter during the sermon, which is always reassuring, thought provoking and challenging. Parents at this mass lead their children by example, gently but firmly explaining the solemnity of the mass and it importance, and the children…oh…they are so precious stumbling through their prayers, exchanging the sign of peace and, for the most part, sitting peacefully, hands folded in prayer.

Nearly everybody sings along with our wonderful choir. It's a proper choir, talented individuals, all, with a passion for sacred music. The choirmaster is a wonderful organist who has peopled his choir with the perfect balance of sopranos, altos, tenors and a booming *basso profundo*. Rumor has it that we even have an atheist as part of the high mass choir because of his great love for sacred music and the way it is properly executed by this choir. If you ever heard them, you would not doubt that this is possible.

All in all, this is a near perfect mass. There are the occasional distractions of a crying baby or a football jersey in place of a collared shirt. Unfortunately, I tend to obsess on these things. If someone is squirming in their seat or not paying attention the way I think that they should be, it breaks my concentration. I begin to lose focus and find it hard to pray with humility, listen attentively and open my heart to the message. So many times in church, if I'm not careful, my mind can drift away to other things, from past love affairs to favorite songs. I don't really believe in all that ADD stuff, I just think that I never made much of a habit of paying attention.

Sometimes I am distracted by the smallest things like lint on the back of someone's jacket or an errant hair out of place on the person in front of me. It is at this time that I close my eyes and do my best to concentrate.

Last week, though, I couldn't escape the distraction. It was audio in nature and try as I might, I was pulled away time and time again by the choir's vocals. The choir's microphones are run through a soundboard to enhance their vocals, to give them a fuller sound, what my band mate would call "wetter". Adding reverb or echo to the vocals makes the choir sound bigger than it actually is, and for a large church like ours, this is practical and even desired.

On this Sunday, however, the reverb was too hot. For most people, this would not be an issue, but as an audio engineer, I wanted to walk up to the front of the church and fix the problem. Most distracting was when the choir came to the end of a phase or a song. Their voices would linger a full second after the note ended in a ghostly echo of the hymn. It was maddening.

I closed my eyes as tightly as I could, hoping that this would somehow keep the audio from entering my ears. I sang louder than usual in an attempt to drown the choir out. All I did was succeed in scaring the little girl in the pew in front of me. By the end of the mass, I was not just distracted, I was angry. Couldn't the choirmaster hear that? Why wouldn't he fix the problem? Was he trying to make us all crazy?

As the final strains of the recessional hymn drifted over my head, I genuflected and crossed myself all the while resisting the impulse to head to the front of the church for an informal technical discussion with the choirmaster. If I did that, I would become like every other old coot with too much time on his hands during retirement. I let my mother out of the pew and quietly followed her to the side exit.

Once we got into the sunshine of God's wonderful fall morning, I noticed a tear on her cheek. I though perhaps she was having trouble with her back again. "Are you alright?" I asked.

"Did you hear it?" she said

"Hear what?

"The angels singing." Her face was full of the joy. She had been witness to something extraordinary. God had allowed her to experience a small bit of heaven. I never told her what I heard, because, honestly, who's to say that I didn't ignore the gift that God offered that day. Angels? Absolutely.

Perfect

"They're perfect," he said. His head lay just below her shoulder, his graying ponytail lying withered on her perfect, white skin.

"What?" she said a little miffed. She was in that delicious state that she loved so much, totally relaxed and near unconsciousness. It happened to her every time she made love and it was as close to perfect as she ever came. She loved that dreamy existence; not like the feeling Zomig gave her when she took it for a migraine. It made her feel like she was trapped in a dream where she couldn't wake up. It lessened the pain of the headaches but left her zoned. It should have been called Zomb-mig. "What are you talking about? She hated being wrenched from her bliss.

"Your breasts!" he said, teasing one of the nipples with the tip of his pinky. It stood at attention almost immediately. "They're perfect!" They hadn't known each other for very long, about six weeks. He asked her to marry him almost right away. He couldn't believe his good fortune, this beautiful woman, willing to talk to him, go out with him, jump into bed with him. He kept waiting for the other shoe to fall. She was so beautiful, she made him nervous and when he was nervous, he said stupid things like "Your breasts are perfect."

Still they had a lot in common. They were the same age, both widowed with kids and both fairly independent. He could see how marriage could work out between them. They both had good jobs; the kids were mostly grown and they held their extended families at arm's length. If he could just be sure that she really did like him and didn't have some ulterior motive for sleeping with him.

"Nice of you to notice. How long have we been together?" She was fully awake now and not happy about it.

"No. I mean it." He worried both nipples plump again and closed one eye, lining them up the way he sighted a target when bow hunting. They were the exact same height. They stayed erect for exactly the same amount of time and then lost their color and flattened out just a bit. He did it again.

"Stop that!" she growled. "What is it with men and boobs? Are you kindred spirits?"

"Haven't you ever noticed? I mean, haven't you ever looked at yourself and thought, "These are pretty nice.""

"I'm not that self absorbed," she said. He breathed on them and watched them turn slightly pink. He wanted to see if they would develop goose bumps.

"It's the first thing I noticed about you."

"I beg your pardon." Now she was awake and insulted. Her hair was obviously her best feature.

"I mean….you know…I tried not to stare, but they're such a part of you. They're the reason I got to know you, because I was trying so hard not to look at them I had to talk to you to keep my mind off of them. The first time I saw them up close, you know, like this, I thought I was going to….I don't know."

"Men are so stupid." she sighed. This was something she had known for a long time. It was one of those sisterhood truths, like the Ten Commandments. "And Shelia came down from the mountain with the tablets and said She has commanded as such: Men are so stupid; Men will do anything for sex; Men are like unto dogs; Men know nothing of love.", etc.

Still, she liked having him around. He really would do anything she asked, although she would never take advantage of him in that way. She was using him for sex, kind of, but you never tell a man that. Then they take their show on the road and try to hump a bigger audience. He was all those things a woman wants in a man. He had a job, a good job and a steady job and he left her pretty much alone. After some of the choices she had made with regard to men, she felt good about this guy. He was sweet and gracious and pathetically eager and he really was a pretty good headache reliever.

"They're not mine, you know," she confessed.

"What?" He was still somewhere in dreamland contemplating a world of perfect breasts.

"I mean...they're mine. I paid for them. I own them." Logic pulled him back from his fantasy. What was he hearing?

"They're fake?" He couldn't believe it. "I can't tell. I mean, how do you know? How can you tell?"

"There's a little scar under each one." He lifted the one nearest to him with the back of his index finger and inspected it. There was a tiny seam. How could he have missed it? He thought he had been over every inch of her and had found no imperfections anywhere. She was smooth and seamless and .....perfect.

"Oh," he said, trying not to act disappointed. "I see. Does it hurt? I mean, did it hurt?"

"Not really. Just a little sore for a week or two, after."

"Why did you?....I mean, why would you want to?..."

"I just wanted to be bigger. I was small all my life. I had no shape. I actually want to get bigger ones." He contemplated this. These were perfect, or at least as perfect as he'd ever seen, until a minute ago. A bigger pair would make her more noticeable. Other men would start to come around. What if she used the big ones to find somebody better?

Worse still, what if something went wrong? What if they got the symmetry screwed up? These were exactly the same size and shape and color. The nipples were exactly the same height. He didn't think he'd ever seen that before on a woman. They were so life-like. What if that changed? "You sure you want to do that?" he asked, "I mean, these are pretty awesome." He felt stupid using the word awesome to describe her as if she were some bar maid.

"Well, yeah. I think I would look better. Don't you?" Was this a trick question? How should he answer? How could he put the best face on this?

"I don't know." He whined a bit. "I'm kind of used to these. I think you look good the way you are. Besides, at your age..." His mind started screaming at him. "Red alert! Red alert! Incorrect choice of words. Begin formulating excuse immediately!"

"What about my age?" She sat up, dumping his head into a heap on the pillow.

"I just meant surgery is always risky…"(ABORT! ABORT! ABORT!) "I just don't want to see anything go wrong."

"Please. It's an outpatient procedure. They do it all the time. It's really my decision anyway." He sat up next to her. She pulled the sheet up to cover herself. He caught a glimpse of them as she tucked them away. They seemed to be waving goodbye.

"I just think that they're perfect the way they are." He heard himself whimper a little bit. "There's no need to tamper with perfection. I guess I'm just being selfish." This must be the other shoe he had been worried about for the past few weeks, except it was his shoe and he had thrown it.

"All men are selfish." was her response. This was another of the ten commandments of women. No matter that they did everything they could to keep themselves attractive, men were never satisfied. Oooh! That was another commandment.

"I'm sorry. I don't know what I'm saying. Your breasts have me confused." OK. Now it was just like words were spilling out of his mouth without any direction whatsoever. How could he fix this? If he stopped talking, he couldn't do any more damage, but if he shut up, he couldn't explain himself. What if he was honest? No. That was never a good idea.

"I'll give you that," she said, "Most men don't have the sense God gave my left boob, and it's artificial. He sat silent. "I've got to get some sleep." she sighed. "Hand me a Zomig out of the nightstand would you?" She turned off the light touched herself and thought "Perfect".

Soccer and the Decline of Western Civilization

About a mile north of Santa Fe, New Mexico on the interstate, is this highway sign:

South 285	**8 km**
Glorietta	**23 km**
Las Vegas	**98 km**

It is the last vestige of a failed attempt to pull Americans down from our center of the universe status. Americans were, in the late 70's, asked to adopt the metric system as used by the rest of the world. Globalist conspiracies aside, this was just not going to happen. This was America, land of opportunity. People from all over the world have come here to flee the tyranny of the metric system and all that it stands for.

The metric system was brought from France in the early 1800's and for most of that century and the next, the US Government tried to bring the American public in line with the rest of the world. We signed the Treaty of Meter in 1875, created a cute logo for the Metric Conversion Act of 1975 but finally disbanded the US Metric Board in 1982.

As should have been expected, Americans sneered at these attempts to make us part of the world community. *"The metric system? Divide everything by ten? How quaint."* But I digress.

A much more sinister project had been underway since the late 1960's. One organization was already indoctrinating the children of Americans with the idea that we were not better everyone else on earth. They would use our children at play to turn the world against us. What was this most sinister cult? The American Youth Soccer Organization, or AYSO.

The AYSO, was created in 1964 in Los Angeles with the goal of getting our children to play the world's game. With their red and blue plAYSOccer bumper stickers and their "Everyone Plays" philosophy, the program became a godsend for every parent with an un-athletic child.

This philosophy, Utopian in nature, promised that children would be part of teams balanced to their skill level so that no child, no matter how awkward or dysfunctional would be allowed to participate for at least half of every game. Never would a child be left out or be taunted by their peers for sucking. In the mid seventies, the first down syndrome player was allowed to participate as a testament to this philosophy. It was a year later that the Special Olympics added soccer to their program. In 1995 the first AYSO program was founded in Moscow. *Moscow! Russia! Hello?!* Was no one paying attention?

The organization now has a stranglehold on the American public with over 50,000 teams and nearly three quarter of a million players. Children and parents are no longer merely encouraged to participate, but are often coerced by peers that vaguely suggest that not participating would be racist, as the world plays soccer. Often, children are encouraged to call this game by its international name, *fútbol.* Some children don't seem to know that football is an American game of tough minded and tougher spirited men. How sad for us.

Parents are promised low cost participation. After all, what do you need to play soccer? Children in most countries have only a pig bladder for a ball and even those children who have lost hands and arms as part of their homeland's civil war are allowed to play because catching the ball is not a requirement. As a matter of fact, catching the ball is AGAINST THE RULES.

The American public was sold a bill of goods. Ask any parent today about the cost of having a child in a soccer program and you'll get a list of required equipment than includes not just the aforementioned pig bladder (The really good soccer balls are about $50.00 and hand stitched by East Indian children that have to work 10-12 hours a day for no little or money. No soccer for them.), but also a uniform, special shoes, goalie gloves, shin guards and helmets. There are also the tournament fees and membership dues that must be paid. Where does this money go? AYSO has only 50 full time employees and a quarter of a million volunteers. I suspect that some of the money goes to support soccer in other countries, but there is no proof of this.

Forty years later; parents who were themselves indoctrinated into this cult now demand that soccer be added to the public school sports curriculum. For them, it is an opportunity to re-live, through their children, the glory days of mediocrity when they were allowed to score a goal, uncontested for the sake of fairness. They want their children to feel this artificial rush of pseudo-victory and never have to feel the character-building sting of defeat. "Finally, a sport that our children can stink at!" In years hence, we have seen the proliferation of other pseudo-sports like T-Ball.

It is guilt ridden American parents who want to show the world that our children are no different than the world's children. But our children are and should be different and better in every way. We are better educated, better financed, better nurtured, better entertained and better disappointed. In short, they should be better prepared for the chaos that is the world.

Part of the problem is the way we have Americanized soccer. You don't have to be good at soccer in America; you just have to show up. Really, if your child can't tie her or his own shoe, that doesn't matter, they can play. Everywhere else in the world, if you fall over your own feet, you're not chosen for a team. Some governments routinely torture national soccer teams that don't make it to the finals of the World Cup. This is one thing that we should adapt for the NFL. Talk about motivation. On the other hand, if you're missing a thumb or hand or an arm but you can kick the ball 200 yards and field a really tough header, you're in.

Helmets and shin guards? C'mon! We are either overly litigious or overly protective, because the rest of the world doesn't use this equipment. Most of the world plays this game without managed soccer fields, coaches, nets or shoes. We have successfully wussy-ized the game so that our kids don't get bruised. No American child is more than a few steps from an asthma inhaler or a reassurance hug from a team mom. At least in little league, the parents go after each other with bats from time to time. The world over, there is no such thing as a game that is too rough. If you are knocked unconscious, you were just showing a little bit of hustle and if you break a nose or someone's last remaining arm, you're just playing with passion.

Worst of all, our soccer is organized. This means kids only play when they are supposed to. They rarely practice, and even then, halfheartedly and once the season is over, it's over. No more soccer until spring. In South America, Indochina, Europe and everywhere else, a soccer game can spontaneously break out at any moment. Kids bounce soccer balls off of their heads all day long. No parents or coaches are involved. Bad calls or someone cheating are settled through fisticuffs, and so you learn another skill.

It's for these reasons that the US now finds itself under the cloud of terrorist threats. Years ago, no one would have challenged us. "You'll take the Marshall Plan and you'll like it!" Now, Americans are routinely harassed everywhere they go. Sure, the citizenry of other countries have always hated us, but never were we threatened. And who's to blame? American soccer.

From this idyllic world, where Americans were untouchable, the American soccer team strolled into the World Cup arena and had their collective asses kicked. These now grown kids, who were never challenged, never got hurt, never practiced and never faced the possibility of losing now faced tough minded, highly skilled players from every country on earth. Without question, even the smallest, most backward, illiterate country without two *kwacha's* to rub together, field intermediate school soccer teams that are more skilled than the American pros. So the result should not have been a surprise. These American players, who had always had this sense of entitlement about soccer shook off loss after loss after loss by saying that Americans had only been playing the game for 40 years and had a lot of catching up to do.

America could no longer hide her vulnerability. Perhaps America was mortal, like everyone else. Maybe she could be beaten in more than one arena. We quickly lost Baseball and Basketball gold medals in the Olympics. Americans were now being harassed at an alarming rate. A simple jaunt to Tijuana was now becoming no different than a trip to the mall. No longer would the merchants haggle over the price of a piece of fruit.

We can fix this. It's not too late. First, we must stop coddling our kids. If we insist on making them play soccer, let's make it as true to the third world play as possible. This means no more managed soccer fields or parental supervision. A glass strewn vacant lot surrounded by traffic works, for starters. No uniforms or safety equipment and for Pete's sake no sucky players. Better yet, let's make them play real sports where the only safety gear is a cup or a mouth guard and where the only rule about fighting during the play is that you can't use deadly force. Next, we stop competing in the World Cup for at least a generation, to clear the palette, so to speak.

Finally, let's adopt the attitude of street-ballers and hockey players everywhere who believe that teeth are mere window dressing and that the more scars you have showing the more cautious the guy guarding you needs to be. After all, it was the US brawlers of 1980 who beat the Soviets at their game, hockey, and brought Olympic gold home. Let's make the world respect us for the mean bastards that, historically, we have always been.

Pod People

I'm going to sue the state school system one day. I'll find a bunch of others like me and we'll file a class action lawsuit on behalf off all those kids that were screwed up by the educational system, or at least the educational system that shaped my thinking.

In the 1970's, alternative education was the wave of the future. What better place to start shaping the future than in Kindergarten and Elementary schools. At the age of 6, we were going to be in charge of our own destinies. We were foot soldiers on to the front lines of the free thinking movement, put there by educator-generals that believed no direction was the best direction.

This was a time when many educators came from the disaffected. People went to college in the 60's without any clear plan. After a couple of years of protest and a half hearted effort to create change through a haze of pot smoke, these college students saw their peers moving off to lucrative careers elsewhere in our capitalist society. Either as a counterbalance to the establishment thinking of the time or as a way of justifying four years of tuition at a state college, these people became teachers. Stupid hippies.

They brought to the table new "alternative" methods of teaching. Children would not be forced to learn, but rather, gently guided into learning. No grades, no competition, no pressure. Each child would be in charge of her or his own education. Each child would learn at her or his own pace without restrictions. Children were to be treated with respect, as peers in the learning experience. Their input would be vital to the whole learning process. True equality would exist within the classroom. All children, regardless of race, creed or ability to learn would be treated with the respect and dignity all people deserved. No child would be placed above any other and every child would have a voice.

There is a pendulum effect that exists in our school system. One school of thought advocates education solving everything from poverty to substance abuse to gang violence. This pushes the pendulum toward freethinking as a way to make learning more accessible. Once this happens, another, more conservative school of thought begins to call for a back to basics type of education, the idea being that every child should learn the same thing the same way at the same time. Kids who can't adapt to this form of education would end up working at McDonalds or in prison, the free thinkers argue. Each time the pendulum swings, a new theory emerges, becoming the next big thing and everybody jumps on the bandwagon. (ref: "No Child Left Behind")

And so, in the 1970's at the apex of the freethinking movement, the open classroom was born. This was an all-inclusive free space where learning would be at the center of a child's experience. Each classroom was less a classroom and more a learning landscape without restrictive walls. The alphabet, artwork, math equations, photos of people from different cultures, colors, animals and any other external stimuli dotted this landscape. There might be bookshelves, bulletin boards or other partitions conveniently placed to half-define a space, but the idea was to empower the children with the idea of no boundaries. We were free-range children bombarded with input no matter where we turned.

Learning stations or "pods" were set up around the classroom. There was math pod, the building pod, the reading pod, the art pod and my favorites, the working together pod and the personal work pod. These last two were meant to teach interpersonal (social) skills and intrapersonal (creative) skills. There was a place for kids to spend quiet time or have a snack and gave you a chance to get away from the learning experience for a few moments. Teachers worked in teams and someone was on call to help any child work out whatever issues may crop up, from bullying to PTSD. Only the music pod was in a separate building due to noise.

Each learning space held up to 120 students at any given time and was divided into groups of 15- 30 students. These core groups would be where discussion of the learning experience would take place and ideas would spring forth. Imagine a hundred elementary school age kids, all yammering on at the same time. For cultural purposes, each group was given a different Native American tribe designation. There was the Navajo tribe, the Cree tribe, the Sioux tribe, the Cherokee tribe, the Potawatomi tribe and so on. Right off the bat, this presented problems.

Because the pod system was all-inclusive, kids with learning disabilities or other intellectual impediments were mainstreamed into our classroom. This meant that kids who suffered from anything from severe hyperactivity to mild retardation were included in the group learning experience. Unfortunately, when it came time to divide into our respective tribes, these kids somehow were segregated as the Potawatomi tribe.

Now, to send kids who are easy targets for jibes and cruelty into a classroom situation was bad enough, but to give them the designation of the Potawatomi tribe was just blind stupidity. None of the kids could identify themselves as being from that tribe, and each day, we took great delight in cornering some poor kid and asking her or him what tribe they were from. "Puh..Puh..Puh.." they would stutter, looking at their shoes. It would have been better to designate them as part of the Cree tribe as about half of them ran around all day involuntarily trilling "Cree1 Cree! Cree!"

Projects went unfinished, discussions went off track despite the teachers best effort to keep us focused and without a grading system, whether or not we were learning was unknown. It was a free for all and we kids quickly discovered that the easiest way to get out of a project we didn't like was to wander off to another pod. For an attention starved kid like me, telling any member of the "team" that I felt bad, would get me quickly whisked away to the relaxation pod where I had the undivided attention of at least two instructors trying to ferret out what was causing my anxiety.

Without competition, those kids who did their best to impress the teachers would get the same praise as someone who put almost no effort into their work. "Look what Marie drew," one of the teachers would say pointing to a few scribbles and some sort of stain on construction paper. "Let's give Marie a big hand." Marie was an idiot. I know. I was there. The upshot was we stopped trying. We'd spend our classroom hours sleepwalking or being as disruptive as we possibly could, hoping to get the teacher's attention.

As a result, I never really learned to focus. I couldn't read well until my sophomore year in high school, thanks entirely to a very attractive librarian with red hair and knee high boots. I got as far as my junior year in High School and when I was in danger of dropping out because I couldn't or wouldn't focus on my required courses, I was moved to Freedom High School, an alternative school for those of us that had grown up outside of mainstream education. Imagine my surprise when some of the teachers I had had in elementary school turned up as staff members at Freedom.

I was given more responsibility at Freedom High. When I complained about the music curriculum, I was handed the class and told, "You're so smart, you teach the class." When I inquired about why the school didn't have a newspaper, my English Skills instructor exclaimed "What a great idea!" and paired me with a red haired girl, presumably another complainer and put us in charge of the school's literary endeavor. If I learned anything at all, it was to keep my mouth shut. I did fall in love with that girl.

After six months of coming to school just to skip out with this girl on the pretense that we were doing some investigative journalism, I was given early release. The credits that I had lacked upon entering the school were miraculously made up and I was even ahead. I remember getting credit in a class that I had never actually attended. I was told that I had received the credit because of my "life experience". My girlfriend, meanwhile, was moved off to New Futures, a school that offered expectant mothers' the opportunity to finish their education.

To this day, I don't focus well on any task. I'm easily distracted. Some might say I have Attention Deficit Disorder or ADD. I just think that this is something I learned a long time ago from well meaning people who believed that, even as a six-year old kid, I would find my way. They provided the light, any number of paths and all the tools I would need. It's just that I was never really told the difference between a hammer and a nail. Either could be a tool. Who was to say what was right?

Sponsor

"Could you talk to him?" she says.

"About what?"

"About how you stopped." She's talking about my drinking. I've been sober 28 years and she'd like me to give her boyfriend advice on how to beat this thing. I don't like him much. He's what I am, what I used to be. He's weak and stupid and manipulative and it would be so easy for me to ruin this thing for him. I'm jealous because she loves him and she should love me. "Sure," I say, "I'll give him a call."

So here I am, listening to this guy try to pull the crap on me that I pulled on people for years. "So, what do you do down there, at work?" Alcoholics always try to get you to talk about yourself so that the focus is off of them.

"This isn't about me, it's about you."

"So how did you stop?" Second attempt. This is an alcoholic's favorite game. Don't get me wrong. I love talking about me. I'm my favorite subject. No one is more interesting than me, but I have to be tough if this is going to work out for her and what's-his-name.

"Short answer? I stopped drinking. How are you going to stop? What sets you off?" He talks about being bored. He talks about being divorced, missing his kids, ruining his relationships with family, friends, employers. He talks about this girl being his salvation. It's like a mini AA meeting. "Hi. My name is blah and I'm an alcoholic. Alcohol ruined my life. Blah, Blah. Waaa, waaaa." I could never get though one of those meetings without being drunk.

"This is my last chance with her," he says. "If I screw this up, she won't take me back." We both know that's not true. She needs him. She needs someone more fucked up than she is in her life to take care of. She needs someone to say, "I need you. You believe in me. No one's ever cared about me the way you do." She needs someone to love her but she believes that no one can love her unless they have to.

"So what's the plan?" I say. "How do *you* stop drinking?"

"Stay busy?"

"And how do you do that?"

"Find work? I called a guy and he said he had work, but then he never called me back. I waited for three days." He wants me to validate his it's tough out there for a drunk attitude or give him an A for effort. I just stare at him. He looks down at his hands, waiting, hoping for sympathy. "I have to find something," he finally says.

Then I just erupt. I can't stop myself.

"You have to get out. You can't live with her. She drinks. You can't be around people who drink. It won't work." I know what I'm saying is the truth. I know what I'm saying is right. I just feel selfish saying it. I don't want him around her. I don't want him to be with her. She doesn't belong with him. She belongs to me. "You have to make your own money, live in your own space, pay your own bills and depend on no one. You need to rebuild your relationship with your parents, your children, your ex-wife and all those people you screwed. I'm not telling you anything you don't already know. You can't feel better about yourself until you're on your own, otherwise, you'll let her take the blame for you not getting sober."

I can't stop myself.

"I know how it's done. You tell the girl you can't cope because you love her so much and you feel like such a disappointment to her because you have nothing but this wretched life to offer and you can't take care of her and she's saving your life, really and only she can pull you out of this mess. But it rarely happens. If you fail, it's her fault for not giving enough and if you succeed, you did it in spite of her."

He blinks at me. He's flushed, trying to subdue his anger. No one likes to be called on the carpet. "Well, thanks man. I mean..,I really appreciate your talking to me. I'll think about what you said and once I get on my feet..." his words trail off.

I feel like shit. I know what will happen. What he told me, I will hold in confidence, but what I told him, he'll use against me. He'll tell her I told him to leave her. He'll tell her I said she's enabling him, making it harder for him to recover. He'll make it her fault. He'll intimate that I don't want her to be happy, that I think that she's better off without him, that I'm jealous.

I am, though. I want her all to myself. I want to fix her, take her pain away, make her understand that she is worth loving. I want to do for her what she wants to do for him. I want to make her whole.

Jazzed

"Jesus, I'm late. I'm in so much trouble." She says. "What's the problem?" I'm puzzled. She regularly works after hours to get things accomplished. We're working on a project together, nothing earth shattering. "It's like....seven o'clock. Does he expect you home at a certain time?"

"No. It's you. He doesn't like me hanging out with you."

"But we're not hanging out. I mean....it's work. It's not like we're having dinner or anything."

"It's....I don't know," she says, "He gets all weird and moody and he won't talk to me."

"Wow. Sorry. I mean....I didn't know. I'll try to be more discreet next time. Less enthusiastic." I say this with conviction, but inside I'm jazzed. I'm a threat. I have crossed that boundary into another man's territory and he actually feels threatened by me. I'm the big dog.

This girl is completely out of my league. Pretty, sexy, smart, bold. She has a warped sense of humor that compliments mine and when I go over the edge, she scolds me while being completely amused by my inappropriate behavior. I have nothing to offer this girl. I could never live up to her expectations. I could never afford the trips he takes her on or the shoes and the jewelry he buys her. Who knows what he's like, personality wise, but I assume he's a nice guy. She couldn't possibly be that superficial.

I suck as a father and I would never have been able to look after her kids, get them through college and such, the way he did. I'm not Chicano enough for her. Not militant enough. Too assimilated.

"No. I mean....I don't know. He knows I like talking to you." She says this with a skosh of guilt in her voice. Not guilt about not telling her husband everything she thinks, but the kind of guilt you feel about having a kinship with someone other than your significant other. Someone who has that component missing from your mate. That thing that would make him or her perfect.

This confirms my theory that all women need at least two men, someone to take care of the mechanical and someone to take care of the emotional. For women, men are a convenience. We take on the tasks that are beneath them. Taking out the trash, so to speak. It's not that these are things women couldn't do for themselves; it's just that there are lesser beings to handle them.

What women need, what women *want*, is for men to listen. They want to talk about everything, from the mundane to the profane. What's important to them is not that we care about what they think, they want to know that we care *that* they think. It's not about content it's about expression. Women vocalize as a way to reason things out in their head. They don't really need input (a rookie mistake made by men) they just need interaction.

Men often talk about how women jabber on about nothing, which, in that context, is true. We sit on the couch with the voices in our head screaming "Shut up! Shut up! Shut up! Can't you see I'm watching the game?" But they're not necessarily looking for advice or logic or even a response. When they hear themselves in conversation, some things that have been tumbling around in their head begin to make sense. It's why women seek out professional listeners, therapists, psychics, book clubs and the like. They want someone to hear them.

This is what makes me so dangerous. I have always listened. In junior high I listened to some girl I longed for talk about how stupid and mean her boyfriend was. While I never got the girl, I got what was important to the girl, and I have used it to my advantage ever since. When women talk to one another, they seem to want validation. "Girl, he so stupid. Uh-huh. I told you so." There is also a sort of competitive edge as to who has the better (or worse) story.

Women occasionally ask the why-do-men-do-this question, but they're really just sounding things out. The answers are already there in their head; they just need to hear what they sound like in the air. And really, what's to "discover" about men? Love us and we'll do whatever women ask. We'll give them our lives and abandon our dreams to help them pursue theirs.

I have spent my life listening, caring, understanding, reacting and providing the one thing that is most important to women. If a women mentions that she likes shoes, or a certain type of handbag, a particular style of clothing or candy or perfume, I file that information away. When a special occasion comes around and the item appears in a gift bag, I know the gift is not the purse or bracelet, but the act of remembering. Any man, who cares enough to listen, is nearly superhuman as far as most women are concerned. When a woman knows that she can call on me anytime and that I will listen to her, she is mine.

At first, I did this to ingratiate myself to women. To get them interested in me, but there was a point where I became interested in them. I find women fascinating. They are completely unique and unduplicated. The combination of beauty and emotion is incredibly inviting. I find their emotional side much more sexy than any physical attribute. The more emotional, the better.

I called her later to tell her how jazzed I was about irritating her husband. Next time I'll call when I know her husband is there with her, just for the extra kick. I am so going to hell.

Love Sick

Insolent little prick. Who does he think he is, stealing my girlfriend like that? What gave him the right?

OK, so I hadn't really been seeing Cheryl regularly for some time and I was sleeping around before we technically stopped dating, but that had nothing to do with him sweeping in and taking her away. There are rules and she still belongs to me.

"Don't they make a cute couple?" her sister says. She never did like me. James is a little taller than Cheryl and older by five years. He's a Vietnam Vet, although he came in at the tail end of the conflict when all that was left to do was deserting the civilians and leaving them to suffer at the hands of the North Vietnamese. Hardly a hero.

I love Cheryl. She's innocent and sexy. She's petite and a little plump, but beautifully shaped. Her skin is smooth, caramel colored and seamless. She has crystal green eyes, wire brush hair and a wonderful laugh. Her voice is deep, erotic and dripping with honey. I love the way she says *Superfine*, her favorite word. Her voice on the phone sets me off more than seeing her in person.

She was the perfect girlfriend. She adored me, did whatever I asked, waited for me to call, never crowded me and loved me any time I wanted her. She knew I had other girlfriends (OK, maybe not to the extent that she knew I was sleeping with them) but seemed fine with my friendships with other women. She had told me once, in that beautiful, sexy voice, "You men have to have your playtime because you think your all that, but you always come home." If we ran into some girl I knew, Cheryl would fade into the background until I finished my conversation, happy just to be continuing on down the road with me.

I swear I tried to ignore her after she told me about James. I just couldn't quit. I talked to her and she said, "Well….you know….it wasn't like we were going to get married or anything. It seemed like you got tired of me. James is nice. He needs me. He's suffering from the Agent

Orange and he has Leukemia and he has a bad heart. Doctor's say he doesn't have a lot of time left."

"So why hitch your wagon to that misery?" I knew it was wrong the minute I said it.

"What do you know about anything?" She had tears in her eyes. "All you know about is you. You don't call. You told me not to bother you so much. What am I supposed to do? Wait for you to get tired of your other girlfriends? At least James appreciates me. Maybe I can make him better."

"Sorry." I was sorry. Sorry I had lost her. Sorry I had taken advantage of her and then tossed her away. Still, I know men. There is no card we won't play to get a woman to care for us. And the sympathy card is the ace in the hole. There's not a guy in the world that hasn't wished for some dreaded disease just so he could use it to get some unattainable piece of ass. "Don't worry about me, baby. It's just the cancer." I knew James wasn't as bad off as he said he was. Proof of that would bring Cheryl back to me.

The first thing I did was shut up about James. I needed information, so I didn't comment one way or another. I left it alone and if Cheryl wanted to talk about him, I listened. The first thing I heard about him was his money situation. How she was helping him out now and then when he had to pay his car note or was short on a house payment. All of his money went to medical care, she explained. Nothing pisses me off more than a man that can't take care of himself.

Now Cheryl doesn't make a lot of money. She works what she calls in that luscious voice "full-part time". Plenty of hours and no benefits. She really can't afford to be paying this guy's bills, but she has always given her all for a chance on love, a flaw in her character I had exploited and it now seemed that James was taking advantage of. I gave money to Cheryl from time to time, but that was to pamper her. "Go get your nails done, baby." That kind of thing.

I've seen James' car. It's an old if well kept Camero Z-28. If he's still paying off the note, than he's been paying on it for well over 10 years. I haven't seen his house, but as a vet, he likely got a good deal on the interest rate on something modest and some of his healthcare must be taken care of by the federal government. I also knew that he had a lump sum payout from Uncle Sam because of his disabilities and a monthly stipend.

I heard about his ailments. He may or may not have had bone cancer. Nobody knows for sure. Now this is something that is lethal, not something you can stave off with a few meds. And his Leukemia was under constant treatment. From what I know about this, treatment sucks the life out of you, makes you useless for days. He also had Bronchitis, but still smoked dope ("…for his pain", Cheryl sighed in that breathless way she has). To top it off, he claimed he was suffering from Post Traumatic Stress Disorder from his time in Vietnam. I'm pretty sure that the only action he saw was in the whorehouses of Saigon. Occasionally, Cheryl would mention how he had come to expect certain things because of these experiences in Vietnam. Pissed me off.

Now, it may seem that Cheryl is, well, not too bright. I think the case is more that Cheryl is naive. It would never occur to her that someone would lie to her. She takes everyone at face value. If you walked up to her with a shaved head and told her you were the King of Siam, she'd give you the benefit of the doubt. It is one of her most endearing qualities.

So here's this guy, using everything in his tool bag to get this girl to do his bidding. If he didn't want to see her, he'd just tell her that he was having a bad day or that he had a doctor's appointment. If he wanted her to come over and cook and clean, he'd explain he was feeling a little weak. He never took her anywhere because he said large crowds made him feel closed in, afraid that his PTSD might kick in so, no movies or concerts or dinners. Of course, if she offered to pay, he would go out of respect for her kind gesture.

Most Fridays, he would pick her up from work and take her home where she'd keep house. In the evening she'd cook his dinner and they'd watch movies until it was time for bed. Monday night he'd take her home so she could get herself ready for work the next day.

In the mean time, I continued to look after her. If she needed a ride somewhere, I took her. If she was bored, I took her to lunch or to the mall and if she wanted to talk, I listened.

She first got a clue while sitting at James' house after a Saturday of cleaning and doing his laundry. The doorbell rang and James, too weak to help with the housework up to this point, leaped from the couch to answer the door. It was some woman who was asking James if he felt like going to the casino for a few hours. It was obvious that they knew each other. Through the half open door, the woman saw Cheryl sitting on the couch. "Oh. Sorry," the woman said, somewhat surprised, "I didn't realize that you had company. Maybe some other time."

Later in the week, as Cheryl relayed the story to me over the phone, I could hear her bewilderment. That velvet, erotic voice was soft now, meek and vulnerable. It made it hard for me to concentrate. She wondered aloud what she ought to do. I offered my opinions as comfort. "Well, maybe he's just confused about what he wants. Maybe he's seeing this other girl because he's afraid that he cares too much for you and doesn't want to admit it to himself."

"Ya think? I mean, do men really think like that?"

"Well, sure. Men's logic is all screwed up. We want someone to belong to us but we don't want to belong to anyone else. And we're always hedging our bets. Once we have one girl, we want another girl. But we don't want to toss away the first girl just in case things don't work out with the new girl. He acts one way with you and he acts a different way around this other girl. I mean, if he were really as sick or stressed, he wouldn't feel like going the casino. And the other stuff, the money and all.....no man wants a woman knowing he's broke or that he doesn't manage what money he has well. It just makes him look stupid."

"You don't think he's sick?" She started to doubt him. Perfect.

"I'm sure he's sick," I said, "maybe not as sick as he says he is. Look, if he starts to get too close to you he can claim that he doesn't want you to have to go through his misery with him and he can cut you loose without your feeling bad about it."

"He said something like that the other day. That he never wanted me to see him… weak." Genius. Evil, but genius.

"Look," I said, "he knows who you are. You want someone to look after. That's why you do his cooking, his cleaning, his laundry. It makes you whole." There was silence on the other end of the phone. "Maybe he wants to get out of this thing with you so it's not your fault. If there's some other girl coming around, he knew it would just be a matter of time until you ran into each other, you'd leave and the problem would solve itself." More silence.

"He seems like he wants me around." It was a plea.

"For what?" I can't let her slip away. "I get it. You want to take care of him the way I want to take care of you. If that's what you want to do, then you'll have to put up with stuff like this."

"You always look after me. Even after……"

"Not your fault. I treated you poorly and it's my own fault you went looking for someone else. I made a mistake and I'll always have to pay for it. You are not to blame." I heard her exhale.

So now, here we are, hips locked together, her sensuous voice, throaty and raspy making that "Uff…Uff…Uff" sound. Her arms are spread above her shoulders, hands grasping mine like she's lost. I'm telling her I love her and how much I've missed her. I look into those brilliant green eyes. She can't see me clearly without her glasses. Still, they pierce me. I want her more than ever.

After, we're lying in bed together, the sun burning into us through the sheer, golden curtain on the western window. The light filtering through the curtain makes her skin glow. I have my arm around her and her head on my chest, her right leg thrown over me. Her skin is smooth, seamless, just as I remember, her hair scratching me just a bit. She is warm and calm. I am comfortable, full of myself. I hear her whimper. "What's wrong?"

"I.....James.....I have to tell him. I have to let him know what I did."

"Sure," I say, "but not this minute."

After a bit, I tell her that I'll go to James and tell him that she doesn't want to see him anymore. I'll pick up the few things from his house that belong to her. That way she won't be embarrassed about being with me and he won't have a chance to make her feel any guiltier than she already does. I'll take care if it.

I stand on his doorstep and wait. The house looks pretty much as I expected. Dirt yard. Landscaping long gone to hell. The sticker on the front door warns me that there is oxygen in use in the house and that no smoking or open flames are allowed. The door opens a crack and when he sees it's me he opens it all the way. He blinks in the bright sunlight. He's shirtless, wearing blue shorts and flip-flops. He has no idea. Oxygen tubes drape from his shoulders and he smells like pot.

"What's up, man? Is everything OK?" He looks up at me and grins that stoner grin.

"I came to pick up Cheryl's things. She's not coming back here anymore." I say it slowly. At first, James doesn't say anything. Things aren't quite registering. Must be good shit.

"She's not here. I mean, she won't be here 'til this weekend. What things?" He's sorting out the conversation out in his mind."

"She left some things here. A watch, a bracelet, some of her laundry. She asked me to pick it up for her." He seems to be catching on and motions me in behind him. I follow him through the foyer and into the kitchen at the back of the house. He's trailing the oxygen tube that snakes its way to a large, dark green tank. There are dirty glasses in the sink and a tray full of prescription medicine on the counter. James sits down at the table, out of breath and puts the oxygen tubes back into his nostrils. He reaches around behind him and cranks the valve on the cylinder until a small white ball floats midway in the tube attached to the valve. A slow, steady hiss comes from the tank.

"This heat, it takes a lot out of me." He glances around the room and nods toward the living room. "I think her watch is in there on the coffee table. Maybe the bracelet, too and she's got a laundry basket with some stuff in it in there." He raises his right arm with some effort and points to the small laundry room just off of the kitchen. I go into the laundry room and retrieve a small, green tote with Cheryl's laundry neatly folded into it. There's a few Tees, gray socks rolled up like armadillos and a few pair of flower print underpants on top of everything else.

I tuck the basket under my arm and head toward the living room and find the watch on the coffee table next to a potted plant. It's one I gave her some time ago. The second hand is actually a separate face that rotates underneath the crystal, which has colorful markings on the edge. Once a minute, the markings on the face and the crystal line up to spell *"I Love You"* before becoming a jumble of lines again. I pocket the watch and spot a small remembrance bracelet next to the TV. "This it?" I ask. James wheezes and nods in agreement. I turn it over and look at the inscription. *"All my love-J"*. It goes into my pocket with the watch. I'll find some reason not to give this back to her.

I start to sidle out from behind the coffee table. I knew before I came up here what I would say to him. I had an answer ready for every response, but he just sits there breathing slowly in and out.

"She's not coming back?" He asks this as if to clarify what I said earlier, to make sure that he didn't hear me wrong.

"No." I say. "She's done. Listen, this has been hard on her, She pretty upset. Try not to call her, OK? " He nods again.

"I'll sure miss her. She helped me a lot, especially on bad days like this. I understand, though. I never treated her right. She deserves better. Better than me and better than you."

I stand there for a second and turn toward the door. "I'll let myself out." I say. I walk into the bright sun. The hiss of the oxygen tank is the last thing I hear as I pull the door closed behind me.

Point of Reference

Doc and Mayme used to visit every September. They would fly in to Albuquerque from St. Albans in Queens, NY on their way to Dick and Mattie Gibson's annual Jazz party in Colorado Springs. This was a big deal, with huge stars like Dizzy Gillespie, Clark Terry, Ray Brown and other Jazz legends attending. You couldn't just show up, you had to be invited. Doc and Mayme would stop over to visit their grandchildren, my stepsons, Hashim and Waleed. For Mayme, a proper woman for whom proper decorum was everything, visiting one's progeny was just good manners. I had proposed to Waleed and Hashim's mother at the age of twenty-five and both Mayme and Doc took me for a walk the day before we got married to let me know what the skinny was.

"You know, we won't be sending our daughter any more money after you're married," Mayme said on our walk. This was a surprise to me. I didn't know Cynthia was getting money from her parents. There were a lot of things I didn't know about Cynthia.

"That's OK," I said, "I'm marrying her for her looks." Mayme raised a well-coiffed eyebrow. She never did have a sense of humor.

Doc was more direct. They had lost his luggage somewhere between La Guardia and the Albuquerque Sunport and the only thing he had to wear was a white, Panama suit. We went walking through my less than middle class neighborhood, this tall lean, black man who looked like a billboard for Cuban cigars and his portly, Mexican soon-to-be-son-in-law. When we got to the end of the block, he put his arm around my shoulder and said, "If you ever raise a hand to my daughter, I'll kill you." And then he grinned maliciously. I thought it best not to joke with him and just nodded. "OK then. Let's go eat!" he said with new enthusiasm.

Doc and Mayme loved their family from a distance. The day-to-day responsibility of raising kids had long ago been left to Cynthia. Their other daughter, Alethea, had no kids and didn't care to have any. After so many years of working and raising two daughters, Doc and Mayme moved on to live their golden years. They were on top of the world. He was a well-respected physician in New York and she the wife of a well-respected physician. Because they were Black, they had overcome many obstacles to get to where they were. Both tried to instill in my boys the need for a good education and in me the best way to bring up their grandsons. I remember Mayme taking me to task for having the kids chop wood for the fireplace. I thought it to be character building, but she reminded me that she and the doctor had worked very hard to make sure that their grandchildren would not have to perform the menial tasks that they had once had to perform themselves. Mind you, when the kids used to visit her in New York she would rub them down with bleaching cream in order to help them blend in more effectively.

Doc and Mayme would talk to the boys about the sacrifices that others had made for them so that they, as young black men, would have opportunities not afforded to people of their generation. But Hashim and Waleed had no point of reference, and so, did not understand the point of the story. They took for granted, as all young kids do, the value of all the rights that have been earned for them. It didn't help that Cynthia saw her parents as elitist, bourgeois snobs. (They were, kind of.) My sons had grown up primarily in New Mexico where many people were more fascinated by black skin than fearful of it. Racism would catch up to the boys, eventually, in adolescence.

Doc and Mayme celebrated their prosperity. They lived in a large house in St. Albans, an exclusive Black neighborhood in the borough of Queens that was home to many great Jazz artists. Their neighbors were people like John Coltrane, James Brown, Count Basie, Miles Davis, heavyweight champion Joe Louis and singer Brooke Benton. Every year, Doc bought his wife a new Cadillac. When they came to visit, he would hand her four or five thousand dollars in cash and say "Knock yourself out, baby," and send her off shopping in Old Town where she would haggle with the merchants over an irregular stone or tarnish on a silver bracelet. The merchants still speak in reverent tones about her. They traveled anywhere they wanted to go, partied with the rich and famous and never looked back on their lives as a young, Black couple living in 1950's America.

Doc had grown up in Mississippi, the son of a contractor who made a reasonable living but also knew that despite his skill and hard work, he would never be allowed the affluence accorded to others in his profession. Doc was tall and thin and a child prodigy. He could read before anyone in his age group and breezed through the only public school available for Black children in his county. His father had told him that he would not be able to put him through college, but Doc was able to work his way through a four year University by the age of nineteen. There were no scholarships for Black students, no matter how intelligent, back then.

He moved to Chicago to go to medical school, working as a chemist for some unsavory underworld characters. He swore that they liked him and offered him lifetime employment, be he knew that he could never become a full member of the *familia* because of the color of his skin.

His first choice was to enter the Air Force as a fighter pilot, but because he was six-foot four, he was too large for the cockpit. After graduating med school, he entered the Army as a doctor at the rank of Captain. He served the required six-year stint and moved to Queens to work in a hospital. That's where he met Mayme. She was an emergency room nurse little more than half his height, widowed with a daughter, Alethea. It was rumored that she was working as a nurse until she could find herself another doctor. Doc and Mayme married in 1950. She quit her job the next day.

Over time, Doc established a private practice comprised mainly of Black patients who would not be seen by or who did not trust White doctors. His reputation as a competent physician grew and over time, he began to attract a more affluent clientele, Black professionals including musicians, artists, actors and the occasional heavyweight champion or two.

Doc's affinity for music (he had once sung in a radio broadcast to Admiral Byrd at the north pole) brought him more and more Jazz musicians as patients. He was discreet about their unique treatment requirements like addiction. He would often treat their wives and girlfriends for social diseases without revealing the nature of the illness, telling them they were deficient in some substance or disguising their treatment as something peculiar to their gender. For this, he won the loyalty of the elite in the profession. Doc and Mayme moved into a large house in St. Albans. Mayme bought a gray parrot and taught it to curse at people she didn't like. Life was good.

During one of his conversations with the grandchildren, when he was trying to give them some sort of motivation to achieve beyond their grasp, I asked him what inspired him to be a doctor. He sat back in the big chair in our living room and told them about the incident that changed his life.

When Doc was twelve years old and living in Mississippi, he was like any other boy his age, not interested in much more than having fun. He had chores at home and his studies to attend to, but all that was simply a means to an end. Once those things were out of the way, he could play.

On one occasion, he noticed a large tent going up in a field on the White side of town. It was being placed there to shelter a free barbeque and political rally for Theodore G. Bilbo, campaigning for his second run for governor in eight years. Bilbo was a proud racist, a member in good standing of the KKK and believed in the "natural inferiority of the Negro".

With little to do, Joseph (That was Doc's given name. I was the only one who ever called him Doc,) asked his mother if he could go and see what the fuss was about. As long as his chores were done, she replied, he could go, but added the proviso "Don't go messing with those White folks. You know they don't want you there and you come home at the first sign of trouble."

And so off to the rally he went. As he described it, it was a mess of noise. A great big barbeque with music and White people coming from all over town to see and hear this man who had been governor of Mississippi eight years previous and wanted to be governor again. There were a number of Black people there as well, just outside the perimeter so as not to be run off by the authorities for "mixing" as they called it. After a time some of the Blacks drifted away, but Joe stayed, finding a soft spot to lie on a mound of hay where he could listen to the music and take in the sounds and smell of this growing crowd.

After more than an hour, a commotion rose from the crowd. The great man was coming. They could see the dust trail from his and several other automobiles off in the distance. Theodore Bilbo stormed the crowd, leaping onto the stage as they cheered and cheered. He was a small man, neatly dressed and he removed his jacket and tie and rolled up his sleeves with a flair that said, "I am one of you." He spoke to them through a sound amplification system that gave his voice a harsh, fuzzy tone that made him hard to understand whenever he shouted. Once the crowd was whipped into a frenzy, he waved his hands above his head pleading for quiet.

"Now I'm gonna tell you why you need to once again elect me a governor of this great state of Mississippi. There are some things that I have left un-finished, and what I have to tell you is vital to the very survival of you, your children and your grandchildren." The crowd remained hushed, waiting to hear the wisdom this man possessed. "Now you see them niggers out there sleeping in the sun?" He gestured toward Joe and some of the men lying in the hay. "Well you just let them sleep. We don't want to wake them, no. If we do that, they're going to start asking for things, expecting the same things that you and I have worked so hard to earn. The very things that have been granted to us by the creator. They're going to demand education. They're going to demand opportunities that rightfully belong to you good, strong, White, Christian people. They're going to want to take money out of your pocket and food out of your children's mouth. They're going to try to make themselves better than you. But they can never be better than you. It isn't in their nature. They don't possess the intelligence to better themselves, but it won't keep them from trying."

He continued. "But if we let them sleep. If we give them just enough so that they don't want to have more, if we give them a little education, a little work and keep them out of our churches and out of our homes, they'll learn where their place is. They'll learn that their place is at our feet." With that the crowd mumbled in agreement. Several of the men in the crowd cast accusing glances toward Joe and his compatriots and almost all of the Black men knew that it was time to leave.

Theodore Bilbo went on to win the governorship once again and later became a U.S. Senator.

"After that day," Doc explained, "I stopped playing. I studied and studied and studied some more. I worked to get out of school and out of Mississippi as fast as I could and I never went back. My mother never understood what got into me and I never told her about that day. Every decision I made from that day moved me toward my goal of proving that man wrong. I did whatever I had to do to become a professional. That's why I play now. Because I earned it." The boys stared at their grandfather, unsure of what to say.

Years later, after Mayme died, Doc took me to Dick and Mattie's Jazz party. His health had declined and he needed help getting around, but I think he actually liked having me there. I sat at lunch, surrounded by the very elite of the Jazz community. I was in heaven. At the same table were Zoot Simms, Ralph Sutton, Ray Brown, Oscar Peterson, Butch Miles, Milt Hinton, Barney Kessel and a young Howard Alden and Terrence Blanchard. All of these guys were Doc's personal friends and they respected him as much as he did them. After finishing a plate of prime rib (Doc loved to eat), he pushed the plate back and looked around the table, enjoying the elite company he was in. He grinned that evil grin he had given me just before my wedding day and said to no one in particular "Screw you, Theodore Bilbo."

Old Fart

I can never leave the house again. I cannot subject myself to the embarrassment of my affliction nor can I bring myself to force others to suffer along with me. No one should have to choose between pity and disgust for my sake. I should not expose myself to the world demanding that people accept me for what I am. I should be hidden away.

Nothing could have prepared me for this. It happened without warning and at the age of fifty, one would think that this is the kind of burden that is carried only by the very aged, but here it is happening to me. It has made me feel tired and used. How can I explain without people running away screaming, perhaps at the thought that this, too, might happen to them, someday.

It was like the first tremor of Parkinson's disease or that forgetfulness that is the onset of dementia. I sat on the couch with my wife, relaxing after dinner, enjoying the domestic bliss that we both work so hard to accomplish. I don't know if it was the remnants of a cold or the dust on the windowsill that caused me to sneeze, but in that split second of release I…how shall I put this… I broke wind!

Horrors! I excused myself, of course. This was an anomaly. Clearly I was in a weakened state due to my recent illness or I had eaten something disagreeable to me. This was never to happen again.

But it did happen again and with alarming frequency. Soon it wasn't just a violent sneeze that would trigger such an event, but anything that required effort from me. If I coughed, I thundered. Laughing created short, staccato burps. Lifting heavy objects caused a long stream of audible stress. Bending over, getting up from the couch and getting into the car all became an exercise in caution. Every ordinary gesture was now planned well in advance and executed in a slow and deliberate fashion. I moved like a Tai Chi master.

At first, I could keep it in house. Somehow my mental ability to separate the territorial comfort of home versus a workplace or other communal environment kept public attacks at bay. Through sheer will, I was able to get through the day without tooting. Eventually, though, this too began to become a challenge. More often I was excusing myself from conversation to find a solitary place for release. I insisted that no assistance was required should I need to move a desk or other piece of equipment. I would be fine by myself, thank you. Better that someone perceived me as being overly macho than so old that I could not control my bodily functions.

I began to see myself as a novelty toy, a gasbag that need only be prodded or twisted in the slightest way to elicit an amusing if juvenile bit of entertainment. Should my condition be discovered, that's what I would become. There would be lunchtime contests of Make the Old Man Fart and office pools to see how long I could go before cracking a rat. My life and any respect I had gained in my long career would go up, phffftt!…just like that. I had to get a handle on this.

I surfed the internet in a attempt to know my enemy. What was it in human physiology that caused this effect? Could this be reversed? I prayed that there was a way out of this for me. At least, I hoped, there would be a terminal condition causing this problem so that when people laughed at me I could stare coldly at them and explain, "My doctor says it's a symptom of my advanced colon cancer. I only have six weeks to live, you know." That would shut them up.

I changed my diet. I existed solely on meat, cheese and whole grains. Salads, fruit or vegetation of any kind was off limits to me. If it grew in the ground, it was my enemy. Better that I should die of scurvy than of embarrassment. I did sphincter contractions while sitting at my desk in an effort to conquer this problem through brute strength. I enlisted the aid of chemicals like Maalox, Pepto-Bismol and Tums hoping modern science had already found a solution for this age-old problem. When that didn't work, I turned to ancient remedies and herbal solutions. I would put this behind me, so to speak, by changing the very core of my existence if need be.

Despite my best efforts, I continued to phoof. The sounds coming from me became more and more diverse. No longer was I confined to mere barking spider noises. There was the fart that rose in pitch as it escaped. There was the slow leak. The shudder. I began to catalogue them in an effort to understand them and perhaps prevent them. I tried to keep track of each sound. Was that a "brrfrrt!" or "braaat!"? Were the louder ones coming after a large meal or were they due to stress? Their sonic identities seemed to correspond with the time of day or the mood I was in.

There were the explosive ones early in the morning just after rising. These had clearly been trapped all night, building momentum as they waited for the dawn to break. Stress related discharge seemed to trumpet itself in protest with loud, anti-social howls. Laughter brought on boastful announcement, almost as if my gaseous anomalies remembered their place in entertainment history. At home, the relaxed atmosphere introduced mellow Jazz-like tones of contentment.

Worst of all, I began to bargain with myself. If I could get through a meeting or social situation, I promised to take myself to a private place and let the wind come forth in all its majesty. I found myself leaning this way and that in my chair to sneak one out or simply for the sake of efficiency rather than excusing myself every ten minutes. Gradually, my affliction began to conquer me.

What would be the next thing to go? My hearing? My sight? Bladder control? Would I stop eating with my mouth closed? Would I start to tuck a napkin into my collar at dinner? What if I started to smell like urine and nobody told me? Would I start to wear plaid? The depths that I could sink to seemed endless. This was worse than any mid-life crisis I could imagine and it could not be fixed with a tryst or the purchase of a sports car. As a matter of fact, the worse my affliction became the more remote either of these options became.

My self-esteem took a beating. It was bad enough that I had other physiological boundaries. I now had to contend with a mortifying burden that announced itself to the world as surely as if I walked the streets shouting "Unclean! Unclean!" I was now closer to becoming that man sprouting hair from his ears riding the scooter through the mall. And from what I had heard, this air assault wouldn't end in death. There were stories of cadavers breaking loose long after the breath of life had left a person's body. This was the most final of insults.

Like the loss of a loved one, I found myself well within the seven stages of grief. At first I was shocked, stunned that this could happen to someone as youthful and vibrant as me. I denied the possibility that this could happen. It must be a symptom of a much larger problem. I struck a deal with myself, promising to move on to better health if the problem would only go away. I suffered the guilt anger, embarrassment and depression that my problem created. All that is left now is acceptance.

What a long, strange trip it's been

I stand here, arms well muscled after countless days in the gym. I assume the position, as it has come to be known, in the small circle that is event security. Feet apart, shoulders squared, arms folded at the chest with a menacing scowl on my face. The position is meant to intimidate anyone who gets too near the stage, to make them think twice about trying to get to the performer. They have to know that there is the possibility of getting roughed up by a three hundred pound plus bouncer, someone who, in all likelihood, does not know the meaning of the word civil.

I wear dark sunglasses and am dressed in a black, fitted t-shirt and black jeans. My hair cropped short, my head swivels slowly from side to side to scan the crowd for potential trouble. Legendary promoter Bill Graham, who first hired me as stage security in 1974 told me at that time that there were only three things I needed to remember: Keep my eyes open; keep my mouth shut and don't get distracted by pussy. He added the qualifier, "…and do whatever I tell you without questions."

I learned this simple formula in my years with the Graham organization and the other tours I have worked over the last thirty years. The only difference now, is that the stage and the audience are smaller. I am working security for the annual Children's Fair and the performers are Scooby Doo and Friends, a cast of young dancers in costume dressed as Hanna-Barberra characters including Fred Flintstone and Barney Rubble.

The dancers don their costumes in a dressing room on the other side of the hall. Each dancer wears a chest harness on to which is attached their character's massive head before stepping into a body suit. The dancers are tiny, none over five-five and must dress in full costume in private so as not to traumatize any of the children who might catch a glimpse of a decapitated Scrappy Doo holding his own head tucked under his arm. This is a written contractual arrangement with additional stipulations that the dancers will only perform the authorized dance steps for the show and that contractor will not use the costumes for purposes other than the authorized stage show. They don't want pictures of Wilma Flintstone doing a hootchie dance or Huckleberry Hound and Betty Rubble doing it doggie style turning up on the Internet.

The costumes are hot and stuffy to work in. Although the show is only twenty minutes long, it is a high-energy program and these petite dancers are performing with an additional sixty pounds weighing them down. Despite frequent cleaning, the costumes smell of weeks of sweat and BO. This, I'm sure is not the glamorous life each dancer had in mind during the long hours of *paus deux*. It is imperative that the dancers get back to the dressing room before they pass out from heat exhaustion.

The audience is a throng of screeching children all under the age of 10. They have been at the Children's Fair for the entire morning and are worked up into a sugared frenzy that only the free Ritalin samples from booth 10 can cure. As we make our way to the stage, each child wants a piece of Scooby and his annoying nephew Scrappy. (Children relate better to Scrappy, with good reason.) They paw, pun intended, at Scrappy's paw as he high fives his way through the throng. The eyes of the parents sparkle with childlike glee as the cartoon characters of their youth fall meekly in step behind Scooby and Scrappy. A top heavy Yogi Bear and Huckleberry hound are nearly toppled by a few back slaps from over enthusiastic parents. I can see this is going to be a problem.

The show gets under way with the dancers in position and the soundtrack blasting "*Rurro Reveryrody!*" in Scooby's voice. A squeal goes up from the gallery and the dancers, led by Scrappy, take over. The dancers move flawlessly in their costumes to the beat of old rock and roll tunes. Despite a few clumsy *jete's*, nearly impossible with giant cartoon feet, the performance is going well. The crowd has become less of a concern for me than the logistics of getting the performers back to the dressing room. I will have to traverse this grand hall the length of half a football field with my charges in tow, trying to get them back to the dressing room before they pass out from heat exhaustion. Every second will count.

The easiest way seems to be by going around the crowd. I call one of the red shirted volunteers over to ask if she can gather a few more people to help me form a human chain off stage left where the actors will exit. She looks at me a bit puzzled. "I'm sure the kids will want to meet with Scooby." No, I tell her. Scooby won't be signing any autographs or taking pictures. He'll need to get back to his dressing room A-SAP.

"But…"

"No buts. Now go and find some more red shirts." With that I go back to planning our escape route. I feel energized, like I did after the destruction of a luxury hotel suite by John Bonham. My job then was to stand between Bill Graham and the hotel management, local police and press until he could get the suitcase full of money open. (A suitcase full of money solves almost any problem.) It was an incredible rush to be in the midst of all that power and money and authority with the fate of Bonham and the tour hinging on my actions or re-actions.

I'm amped as I run contingencies through my head. What if the kids break through the line of volunteers? How should I handle an irate parent? What if the elevators are delayed? The solution to each question seems to be the same as it has always been in these situations, keep moving.

I look to my left and see the dancers starting to tire. We're nearing the end of the program and I wait to hear the out cue over the sound system. The volunteer returns with a half dozen other semi-confused red shirts. "This is all I could get. Everybody else is manning a booth or watching the door for pedophiles."

"Not good," I mutter. I'll have to change my plan of action. "Here's what we need to do" I begin to explain. Most of the red shirts at my disposal are only a few years older than the kids in the audience and are transfixed by the stage show as well. They are clearly not taking the threat seriously. I press on.

"We need to form a ring around the characters and keep the kids and parents at arm's length. I will lead the troupe and move the kids out of the way." The volunteers are only half listening and the kids are now at critical mass. From the speakers I hear *"Scooby Rooby Roo!"* We're on. The dancers take their bows and head stage left. The volunteers help them find and negotiate the stairs. We begin to move toward the back of the hall.

As the characters leave the stage, the kids start to close in. One thing I hadn't counted on is a seven-year-old child's lack of fear. Back in the day, when I had to confront an over zealous fan or a jilted "girlfriend", all that was usually necessary was a stern glance that said, "I'll kick your ass right now!" Even a stoned junkie understood that message. Kids, however, are a different animal. As we begin our march around the periphery of the hall, the kids flood by me. They rush through my outstretched arms like subway riders through a broken turnstile. The parents stand back and let the kids race toward us, some encouraging the more shy children to get in and mix it up. The volunteers are no help at all, reveling themselves in the celebration. We sally forth.

Scooby taps me on the shoulder and I lean in toward the massive head with the psychotic grin. "I'm getting dizzy." I hear him say. As I look over my shoulder, it is apparent that the rest of the characters are somewhat disoriented. I begin to try and gently move children out of my way, but they are fluid, swirling gently off of my arms and moving beyond me to their costumed heroes behind me. We are halfway to the elevators and the crowd shuffles alongside and behind us, hoping for more. The dancers are valiant in their attempt to satisfy every child. The barrier between children, parents and the volunteers has completely broken down with the red shirts beginning to fade into the sea of children like shipwreck survivors in their life jackets.

I raise my voice a little. "Pardon me. Excuse me. Ooops, sorry little guy." The kids pay no attention. I'm making progress, although slowly, leading the pack with kids grabbing onto Scooby and Scrappy's tails trying to get their attention. Some parents shout "Slow down" and "Wait", hoisting their little ones onto their shoulders. Almost there.

When we reach the elevator, the doors pop open as if on cue and the characters squeeze themselves into this box designed not for them but for normal sized humans. I stand at the door and announce "Thank you! They'll be another show at two-thirty." There is a collective groan once the doors close. I rush up the stairs like a fugitive and meet the elevator just as the characters start to dislodge themselves from the elevator. Some volunteers that have been taking a break in the dressing room help the dancers through the door. Despite the fact that the expressions on the costumes remain fixed, the body language of each character screams exhaustion.

Once safely in the dressing room, the heads are removed from each of the costumes. Steam pours from each cavity as the sweat soaked and weary dancers collapse onto the costume trunks. They step out of their body suits and release their harnesses, letting them drop to the ground. Towels and bottled water are handed to each dancer.

"Jesus, I thought I was going to die!" say the girl who was Scrappy Doo. She chugs her water and in seconds, her towel is soaked. "I have to get out of these dance skins."

"I was suffocating" another chimes in. "I never knew what that felt like. It's horrible." There's a knock at the door. I crack it open just a little to make sure it's not a tiny fan hoping to get an autograph. It's the promoter. "Some of the parents said you were shoving their kids around?"

"Not a chance", I say. I might have moved a few kids out of the way, but I didn't shove anybody."

"Well, I'm getting complaints." I don't know what to tell him. I explain the situation. These dancers have to perform in an airless environment carrying the equivalent of another person on their back. That they have to get back to the dressing room before they pass out. The stage is too far away from the dressing room. But like all of the promoters I have ever worked for, he's just worried about having to give some of the money back. I listen as he gives me a stern warning. He can't scare me. I toured with Led Zeppelin.

The performance is repeated twice, each time with a little more success. When the day is over, the dancers get their hard earned money, the kids and the promoter are happy and the costumes go back into the trunks ready for the trip to another carnival, state fair or community event.

If I had to compare, I'd have to say that this show was no less arduous than any other I've done. I have had to throw drunks off the stage and pull an artist's head out of the toilet and get him cleaned up and on stage. I have had to lie to wives and girlfriends and boyfriends about the whereabouts of a band member. I have had to take the blame for crimes that didn't belong to me. But nothing has been as surreal as making sure that when I pulled the head off of Scooby Doo or Snaglepuss that the person inside the costume was still alive. I think my event security days are done.

By the way, if you happen to find some pictures on the Internet of Yogi bear inappropriately touching Boo Boo, I had nothing to do with it.

Sid

Sid had seen this before. It was part of the nine years he had spent in a crate as a breeder for the puppy mill. That whole experience, the confinement, the horrible smell and the even more horrible people had done something to him. Worst had been the noise, the constant clamor of yips, barks and growls, howls of desperation, whimpers and the sharp report of people shouting above it all. Sid was not a normal by any means. He was afraid of everything all of the time, but who could blame him.

He had seen this happen again and again, the shallow, rapid breathing and then the stillness. At the mill, he had seen it in newborn pups that had stopped feeding or were pushed away by the litter until they starved. He had seen mothers that had had one too many litters just give up and he had seen seemingly healthy males just fall over and breathe themselves into the awful silence. It had always made him feel ill at ease.

One day, something changed. There were people shouting, but it wasn't the voices of the men and women who always came with food or to pull him out of his crate or take a lifeless pup away from a wailing mother. These voices were new. There were shouts of "No!" and "Get back! Get away!", commands he recognized, but they weren't directed at him. They were directed at the people who had created this chaos. And then there was one single voice above the din, a woman at his cage talking in soothing tones. He began to turn quickly in circles in his crate and to shiver the way he always did when they came to get him.

This woman reached into the crate for him, pulled him out and clutched him to her body, stroking him and talking softly to him. It was nothing like the rough treatment he was used to. Ordinarily, he would have been pulled out by the scruff of his neck and shoved into smaller crate. He would be taken to a cage where a passive, worn out female would be mated to him. Now, the woman carried him to a brightly lit trailer where another woman examined him from nose to tail. They bathed and brushed, fed and watered him, all the time talking in calm even tones. They put him in a clean crate with his own water and a pad to lie on. Sid continued to tremble and the lack of noise confused him. No good could come of it.

As the day wore on, more and more of his compatriots ended up in the trailer. Some scents and barks he recognized and some he didn't, but the familiarity of the situation made him feel more at ease. The trailer began to move and it startled him, but soon, the events of the day put him into a deep sleep.

When Sid awoke, the sun was spilling through the window warming the air just a bit. There was a fresh bowl of food and a soft, round object in the crate with him. He could hear the sounds of people, speaking in the same calming tones he had heard the night before, but none of the words were directed at him. People were talking to each other. He lay as still as possible with his eyes open trying to understand where he was and what these people wanted of him. He dare not move, or they might hear him. He grew tense, the muscles in his neck cramping and his eyes becoming strained from trying to look at things without moving his head. He picked his head up just a bit to ease the cramping and his nose nudged the round thing. It jingled.

This caught the attention of one of the women in the trailer with him. She turned her attention to him and spoke. Sid immediately backed into the furthest corner of the crate, turning and shivering again. He peed. The woman reached in, patted him on the head and spoke to him again. She closed the crate door and draped a sheer cloth across the front. This made Sid feel a little more at ease and he moved forward, away from the puddle he had created. When he was sure she was not coming back, he drank as much water as he could and nibbled on some of the food, taking a mouthful at a time and retreating slightly from the bowl so as not to be caught unaware if the door opened again. After a while, his shaking stopped. He lay back down, closed his eyes and drifted off to sleep again.

He awoke to the sound of this woman's voice again, speaking to him through the cloth. He sat up and backed away. She removed the cloth and opened the door, reaching in with both hands and gently lifting him out. She held him close and walked him out into the fresh air. It was blissfully quiet and it scared Sid a little. The woman clipped something around Sid's neck, surprising him and set him on the ground. He stood rock still. The pads of his feet hurt. He had never touched the ground before. She moved forward a little and gave a tug to the leash tied to his collar. Sid resisted, afraid of where he might end up. People had come and taken the still dogs away and they never returned. Who knew what might happen to him?

The woman urged him forward, a bit at a time. Sid began to pace back and forth to the end of his leash, panting and looking for an escape route. But where would he go? Nothing outside of his crate was familiar. After a while, he sniffed something familiar. Someone else had been there before him and he stood over the spot and peed in greeting. The woman squealed with praise and Sid jumped back with a start. He began to pace again and then he had that stirring that always came after he relieved himself and so he relieved himself again. The woman squealed again. She rolled the round thing toward him and he jumped away from it. She retrieved the round thing and gently pulled him back toward the trailer. She scooped him up in her arms and returned him to his crate. The soiled pad had been replaced with a fresh one and his water and food dish were replenished.

He woke up the third morning to a man reaching into his crate. He brought him out and laid him onto a cold table where a woman gently but firmly hugged him around his neck. He felt something sting his leg. Then he felt the stillness coming over him. This was it. He was going to the place all those other dogs had gone. He tried to hold his head up, but he couldn't move and he passed out. When he woke, it was as if he weighed as much as every dog in the world. He was sore and he had a collar around his head. Maybe he was nothing but a head now. He passed out with a whimper.

When he woke again, he could feel his legs and his tail and he was thirsty. Someone had placed a bowl of water in his crate. He pulled himself to his feet and felt a sharp pain between his hindquarters. He drank until he couldn't drink any more and then he discovered a small amount of food, which he ate. It made him nauseous.

After a few days, the collar came off and it was back to the routine of eat, sleep and go outside. The pattern repeated itself for how long Sid didn't know. He found that he liked the nighttime best and the quiet was something he began to enjoy. It meant that no one would come and he could eat and drink at ease. He could distinguish individual barks from those in the crates near him. He began to hear a change in their demeanor from desperate to cautious to calm.

A parade of dogs came and went, making Sid feel uncomfortable. Then one day some new people came in, a man and a woman. The woman reached into his crate and took Sid out and held him. He began to shake. She spoke calmly to him, and took him out to a smaller vehicle where she put him into a crate. Sid huddled, once again, to the very back. They drove for hours and arrived someplace new, not like the trailer where he had stayed before, but larger.

The women reached into the crate and took Sid out and carried him into the new place. There were two large dogs there that seemed to be happy to see these people. They barked and jumped and tried to get a look at Sid. After a bit, the woman sat on the floor and let the dogs come closer to him. They both gave a series of curious sniffs and the larger of the two barked once, but was quickly hushed by the woman.

With nowhere to run, Sid huddled close to the woman. After a while, the dogs lost interest in him and she set him on the floor. It was soft, not like the hard ground outside the trailer and not like the floor of the crate. Sid quickly retreated to the woman's lap. They sat that way for a while and then she took him outside, placed him on the ground and stood watching him. He stood still looking up at her. She waited, talking to him the whole time. He finally spread his back legs and peed where he stood, which seemed to excite her. She scooped him up into her arms and took him back into the house.

Sid spent the next few days sitting close to the woman and trying to be as invisible as possible. He only ate and drank when no one was looking. He let her carry him outside to do his business and he avoided the other dogs as much as possible, although they seemed pleasant enough. He wanted to go back to that crate with the cloth over it and the quiet nights.

Then yet another change. New people came to the home and made a fuss about Sid. They had a small dog with them who looked like him who barked ferociously at everything and everyone. The people talked to one another while the woman introduced Sid to the new couple. This new woman spoke gently to Sid, stroking him and scratching him under his chin, which he liked.

After a short time, the man picked up the little dog and the woman carried Sid out to another vehicle. They all got in together and Sid remained on the woman's lap. They began to drive, with the smaller dog trying to nudge Sid out of the way. The sun shone through the window of the car and after a while Sid felt warm and fell asleep. When he woke, they were at a new home with new smells and new sounds. The woman put Sid down onto the floor and Sid immediately hid under a small table. He could smell the little dog everywhere and another dog that he couldn't see. He lay under the table while the people talked to him and finally, ignored him.

Come the night, the man carried him outside. While he was taking care of things, he got another whiff of that other dog, but couldn't find him. They brought him in and everyone got into a large bed for the night. The darkness and quiet made Sid feel a little better. The small dog huddled next to the woman to keep Sid away from her so he scooted up next to the man.

Days came and went. Sid had his own bed, which they placed under the table so he could hide. The little dog began to pay more attention to him, cleaning his eyes and ears. He had plenty of food and every night they all slept together in the same bed. There was a small door for him to go in and out of the house at either end and he was left alone for hours at a time with no one paying him any mind, which he liked. He began to follow the small dog around, getting to know the ins and outs of the home. He had his own space and little by little began to venture out from under the table to wander on his own. They took him regularly to have his hair washed and trimmed and to another place where a woman poked and prodded him and insisted on lifting his tail.

Gradually, Sid began to understand that these people belonged to him. He rode with them in the car for no particular reason that he could see, as they always came back home. There was always food and water for him to share with the little dog and a biscuit every evening before bed. The couple did their best not to alarm him, but always made him go out at regular intervals, shooing him out of his bed. He enjoyed having a companion. He followed the little dog around because he seemed to know all of the signals better than Sid. After a time, he began to understand the subtle cues that meant that they were going for a ride or that it was time for bed and he began to let himself out. His routine helped him feel more at ease.

But now, here he was watching this family that he had adopted in a tense moment. They had let the prodding woman into the house and she had talked to the little dog for a moment. The man and the woman were upset, as best as he could tell. They had been that way for he didn't know how many days. It started when the little dog stopped cleaning Sid's eyes. He just lay there all day, not wanting to eat or go out or play. Sid had prodded him a few times, but the little dog just looked at him with tired eyes. There was an uneasy, familiar feeling to that look that Sid remembered that look from a long time ago.

The prodding woman moved away from the little dog on the couch and now the man picked Sid up and set him next to the little dog. The man and the woman sat on either side of the little dog, stroking him and talking to him with shaky voices. He noticed that the little dog was breathing rapidly, his eyes closed and Sid knew that the stillness was coming. He nudged the little dog again and whimpered a little, and then the stillness was there. This caused the woman to moan terribly.

She clutched the still, little dog in her arms. The man ran away. Sid growled at the prodding woman. After a few minutes, the woman put the little dog on the couch and wrapped him up in the blanket from the little dog's bed. The man returned and carried the little dog away. The stillness was the same, but something was different.

A million miles ago, someone would have come along and dragged the little dog out of a crate and tossed him carelessly into a sack, never to be seen again. Here, these people were affected by the stillness in the little dog. They cared about him, just the way they cared about Sid. The little dog was part of them the way Sid had begun to feel a part of them.

Later that evening, Sid went into the back yard. He could smell the little dog, but couldn't find him anywhere. He went over to a corner of the yard where he had once looked for another dog so long ago and he found a patch of new dirt. He went back inside and up the soft, padded ramp to the bed the man had put up to help Sid and the little dog get up and down. He found the woman lying awake. He rested his chin on her hand. She patted him, sighed, pulled him close to her and cried.

Lunch Hour

He stood over her and briefly stroked her long hair with the back of his hand. He remembered it as blonde and radiant for all of those years. It was now brilliant platinum silver, but it had lost none of its silkiness. She breathed steadily and he let his hand continue on to her cheek. The corner of her mouth twitched just a little in her slumber. He reached out with one ragged finger and ran the tip of it down the bridge of her nose searching for the tiny bump that had once been there. She had always hated it and had had it removed at the first opportunity, but he missed it so. With that brief touch, he communicated a lifetime of love. He thought that he saw her smile.

The girls, her daughters, stood in the doorway of this warm and comfortable if sparsely furnished room and watched. They knew him, vaguely. He had been to their parent's home a few times when they were very young and he had been at their father's funeral. Then, he had waited until the long line of mourners that had come through offering condolences. He had gently led their mother off to a quiet corner of the church to speak privately with her. Their mother had hugged him for a long time after the conversation and the girls had put it down to the culmination of a long, stressful day of grief. They thought that he must have been a friend of their father's, but now they understood it to be something more.

The daughters queried one another as to who this man might be? An ex-husband? Their mother had been married once or twice before she had met their father, but they were sure she had not kept in touch with any of her previous spouses. In fact, she had downright toxic feelings about one of them.

The old man seemed comfortable being there as if he was used to taking care of their mother. His focus was entirely on her, oblivious to the rest of the world. The woman stirred a bit and he pulled his hand quickly away, as if he had received a shock. Her nightgown was a whisper of thin, white cotton. Her face would not allow one to determine her age and her skin was still flawlessly smooth where her shoulders peeked through the ties of her gown. Only the tiny wrinkles on her neck and hands betrayed her. Her lips were dry and her breathing slightly irregular. She looked as if she had been sleeping for only a night, waiting for morning to revive her.

The old man was dressed casually, but appropriately for a visit. His clothes well worn but well kept, tailored Levi's and a JC Penny shirt. His skin was tanned and weathered around his large frame and sagged in all of the usual places for a man his age. His hair was thin and combed straight back, his beard gray and he was a little bent. He moved slowly, carefully, perhaps to avoid some pain or because it was the only mobility he had left to him. When he smiled, it was reflected in his soft brown eyes and the corners of those eyes wrinkled with honest joy.

He stood and stared at her for the better part of an hour, until standing appeared to become difficult. He turned and asked if he could sit and, with the girls' approval, lowered himself slowly into the vinyl armchair and watched her some more. He sat back, filling the big chair, the top of his head reflecting the late afternoon sunlight that tumbled through the south-facing window. She did not stir again and he started to drift off a bit, nodding now and then back into consciousness.

When would the visiting hours be over, he asked. "There are no restrictions here." the oldest replied. He could come and go any time as long as the family approved. With that, he stood and announced that he would be back. The girls, though curious, didn't see any harm in letting him visit. In fact, when he had arrived and announced himself as a friend of their mother's, they welcomed the opportunity to have someone sit with her while they tended to their families and other visiting relatives and there was a nursing staff available should any problems arise.

The old man ambled off to the restroom and then to the nursing station to inquire about the nature of the woman's illness. A graying, cheerful black woman in an equally cheerful Snoopy print smock informed him simply that time had finally caught up with her. "Time and age." she said. "None of us can outrun old man time."

"She didn't just lie there and wait for the reaper, though, no, no." she observed, "She had better things to do…went on with her life. She was out running errands and collapsed. She didn't get that beautiful family just sitting around." she said, nodding toward the waiting area. "But now, it's time for her to go home. That's whey she's here at hospice, where her journey from this life into the next can be a comfortable one, like riding the parlor car on the train to glory. Are you family?" she asked with some amount of suspicion.

"Just an old friend." he admitted, emphasizing the word old. "And knowing her, she'll be riding the club car." Some people were just born caregivers, he thought of this woman, feeling a little racist for noting that were an abundance of black women who worked in nursing and that they always seemed more caring than the white nurses he had met. Even his ex-wife, who was black and who had a bit of a phobia about sick people had become a home healthcare worker after they split up 30 years ago.

This woman believed every word she spoke about life and death and heaven to be the truth. "Well, as long as it helps her get to where she's going with love, I suppose it's alright for you to stay." With that, she turned her attention to dimming the lights on the floor for the night. By now the sun had long set and the extended families of the patients were beginning to drift off to put their children down for the night and get some long overdue rest. Only a small staff and immediate family members who volunteered for the night watch remained.

He wandered off down the hallway and around the corner and returned briefly with a single rose in a small glass vase from the gift shop. He cautiously entered the darkened hospice room and asked if he could sit with the woman for a while.

"Will you be alright if we leave for a few minutes?" one of the daughters asked.

"Sure. We'll be fine." he said.

He sat in the chair facing the hospital bed. She lay with her torso slightly elevated so he could see her face reflecting the sparse light from the streetlamps that now filtered through the window glass. It reminded him of the brightest moonlit nights he had seen as a young man and it suited her, even tonight. He closed his eyes, remembering bits and pieces of his life with this woman. There were snapshots of her in high school, at her wedding, at lunch, in the hospital pregnant with her second daughter. He had mourned the loss of so many memories in his lifetime but these were some of his most precious and it seemed as if they had been the first to disappear from his memory. Only the terrible, humiliating, degrading things he had done in his life were clear.

He couldn't remember the first time they met. He could, however, remember what he was like then, a pudgy cherub of a boy with a smooth face desperately trying to get the attention of other people. He had been the background to those people that mattered, a pariah willing to submerge his personality for the chance to be attached to someone else with a better rap. Pretending to be the rebel without having the courage to rebel against anything.

He did remember that when she spoke to his friends, she included him in the conversation as if he belonged. Girls never did that unless they wanted something and even then they were discreet so as not to be attached to him in any way. From that moment on, he was attracted to her because she gave him the thing he craved most, the feeling that he mattered.

Through the remainder of high school, they were friends, he the confidant, she the confessor. He listened to her talk about her family, her boyfriends and girlfriends. She asked him questions about why boys were the way they were, always disappointing her in the end. He did his best to make up answers he thought would satisfy her and make himself sound sympathetic at the same time.

He was the touchstone to which she could return time and time again for advice, sympathy and love. It was a role he deeply enjoyed. It made him seem less the outcast and she never turned her back on him the way others sometimes had, avoiding him in certain social situations. In fact, she defended her friendship with him and even introduced him to her family. They even went out on a few dates.

As high school ended and other lives began, both moved on, he more confident in his ability to socialize with the opposite sex and she more equipped to deal with the world on her own. They continued to date, off and on until careers and other considerations pulled them apart. She was way out of his league and he knew it. He could never give her the things she wanted from the material world and he couldn't stand the thought of losing her to someone else. It was more the losing that bothered him, the fact that he wouldn't measure up in her eyes if compared to another man. He slithered away.

They had made a connection, though, and had kept in touch over the years. He called her, periodically, wherever she lived and no matter what kind of situation she was in, single, married, divorced. They remained attached by this slim thread of need for a friend that would not judge their actions or intentions. They talked to each other without condemnation. He knew her intimately and yet was detached enough to counsel her on the things that concerned her. If he lied about his life, she let it go and if she made some obvious mistake in judgment about someone she loved, he sympathized but never scolded. He always knew when she was feeling bad, even at a distance and she always knew the right thing to say to cheer him.

Over decades, marriage, families, careers and the details of life kept them busy. They both came home and almost by accident, bumped into each other at a local restaurant. Later, they met for lunch and spent hours catching up and reminiscing about their high school days in a wonderful conversation that re-energized their friendship. They had tried including their respective spouses in the relationship, double dating, as it were, but nothing quite satisfied them as this one on one time. During lunch they could be themselves when talking about family or work, life, love or loss. They could be frank with one another about their personal failings.

They eventually settled into a small French bistro about once a month. Here, they found a home. The staff knew them and what they preferred. They rarely ran into business associates or friends. It was time that they could spend with each other that would remain uninterrupted until they decided to get on with their day. It was this pause that many people seek but never find.

Each month, the anticipation would grow in them as they searched for a time when they could meet. He enjoyed being seen with this beautiful woman, never explaining who she was and over time, he rearranged his schedule to coincide with hers so as to not miss an opportunity to have lunch. If conditions warranted, they would meet more often, but never skipped a month. There were no gifts involved, no displays of affection, no future plans made, just conversation. It was splendid. But as with all things, this came to an end.

What should have happened was some sort of disagreement, some argument that drove them apart. Even more appropriate would have been family concerns like the need to look after an ailing family member, a career change or even a jealous spouse putting an end to these suspiciously delightful lunches. What really happened was much simpler. The bistro closed.

They found themselves one day in an empty parking lot, staring at a closed sign that should not have been there. Was it a holiday? Had they got their dates mixed up? Had the cook had a death in the family? It was unsettling. Where were they to go? The anticipation of this day was replaced with frustration and longing. No Earl Grey in white china cups, no quiche of the day, no fresh rolls. Who was responsible? Someone would hear from them.

That afternoon, they settled on a café down the street. It was wholly unsatisfying and cut short their conversation as they mulled over a menu that seemed to offer nothing appealing. They left lunch unrequited and disappointed with their situation. He would get to the bottom of this and all would be put right. They would re-schedule as soon as he had some answers.

Unfortunately, the answers were unpleasant. The bistro had gone bankrupt. Chef had married a woman who had spent all of his money and charged even more to the bistro's accounts. There was no digging out of a hole like that. There was talk of staff buying the place and re-opening, but that never happened. The bistro would not return.

Spoiled by service and a menu that suited their conversation, they went searching for another place to hold their lunches. They began with other small, elegant places nearby her office, desperately trying to find someplace that suited them, but there was always something that was not right. It was often the smallest of things like a wobbly table, flies in the window or the wrong brand of tea. They expanded their search to include Italian and Greek cuisine and finally diners to no avail. It was like trying to have a conversation in a shopping mall.

Finally, it happened. They skipped a month. The excuse was something that seemed legitimate at the time, a family vacation. From then on, it became smaller things, work conflicts and birthdays and money. Neither cared to try and make yet another uncomfortable atmosphere work. Neither wanted to take the blame for not being able to find someplace where they could be together as they once were, as friends in intimate conversation.

It took about a year, but the lunches finally stopped altogether. There were occasional notes to one another, but nothing approaching those wonderful lunches. And now, here he was sitting next to her and missing all of those years they could have had together. How could he make that up? How could he ever be redeemed?

He stood up and again he touched her hand. The oldest daughter sidled up beside him. He hadn't noticed before that she looked remarkably like her mother in middle age, youthful and stunningly beautiful.

"Do I know you?" she asked.

"Sort of." he said. "We had lunch together, you, your mother and I, when you were about eleven." She searched her mind for the occasion. "I brought you tickets for a concert and your mother insisted you come along to lunch so that you could thank me properly." There was a hint of recognition.

"Did I?"

"No. You played with your food. Your mother was annoyed, but she let it go. What happened to her?" he asked, switching gears.

"It's her heart." she said somewhat wearily, the youthful beauty vanishing from her face for a moment, replaced by sorrow. "She was out shopping and she got dizzy and couldn't catch her breath. They thought it was a stroke, but by the time they got her to the hospital, she was unconscious. It's something I don't understand. She was always so energetic. I got on a plane and came right home, but she was already like this."

"So, she's not going home...you know, for her last days?" he asked, knowing the answer.

"I'm afraid not. How did you find out? Who told you?"

"I just knew. Your mom and I...we always had this thing...this connection. I knew something was going on, but I didn't know what. I called your uncle and asked if anything was wrong and he told me she was here."

He reached out with his index finger again and touched the back of the mother's hand. Her eyelids fluttered and the daughter let out a barely audible gasp. Her eyes opened dreamily and she smiled to see her old friend standing there with her. She slowly took in her surroundings. Her daughter's eyes began to tear up and she sobbed quietly so as not to break the silence of the moment. A few other family members came into the room trying to discern what the problem was.

The woman in bed directed her smile toward the old man. She tried to speak, but her parched throat made the words inaudible. He took her hand in his, bent forward and put his ear to her lips.

"I knew you'd come." she whispered. His eyes glistened. "Will you stay for lunch?"

Acknowledgements

I could not have written this book without God's patience. He continues to bless me despite my corrupt nature.

Many people have encouraged me. First and foremost, my mom, Margaret who always believed that I could be more and my late father, Chuy, who spent money on me as a kid even though he didn't understand how anyone could make a living with a guitar; my sister Juanita who taught me how to write poetry; my sisters Rosalinda and Barbara who believed their big brother could do anything and my late brother, Pat, who was the most interesting person I've ever met.

I also want to thank my son Kurt, who continues to challenge me as a father, despite my being absent in his life for so many years as well as my boyz, Charlie, Amigo and Sid, who taught me the meaning of unconditional love and that I am not the most important thing in the universe.

My friends, Nathan, Kristina, Alison, Bill, Lynda, Will and Susan (who challenged me by forcing me to write an erotic story which will *never* see the light of day) for reading my stuff and never lying to me even if they thought something sucked.

My publicist Linda, who reminded me that there is absolutely nothing unique about me and that I had better bring out the big guns if I wanted people to read my book.

Bob Grant, creator of s*peakwithoutinterruption.com*, a website for writers. Bob contacted me out of the blue and asked if I'd write for him. Until then, I hadn't done any creative writing in nearly twenty years.

Finally, all of my friends and acquaintances who know they're at risk of becoming a character in one of my stories. If you see some of yourself here, it's because I think you're interesting.

Made in the USA
Charleston, SC
22 September 2012